12-17-7_ ___
Reread-   Y0-AGV-648

A
Harlequin
Romance

OTHER
Harlequin Romances
by ELIZABETH ASHTON

1373—THE PIED TULIP
1421—PARISIAN ADVENTURE
1453—THE BENEVOLENT DESPOT
1534—COUSIN MARK
1636—FLUTTER OF WHITE WINGS
1659—A PARADE OF PEACOCKS
1713—ALPINE RHAPSODY
1741—MOORLAND MAGIC
1762—SIGH NO MORE
1788—ERRANT BRIDE
1810—THE ROCKS OF ARACHENZA

Many of these titles are available at your local bookseller, or through the Harlequin Reader Service.

For a free catalogue listing all available Harlequin Romances, send your name and address to:

HARLEQUIN READER SERVICE,
M.P.O. Box 707, Niagara Falls, N.Y. 14302
Canadian address: Stratford, Ontario, Canada.

or use coupon at back of book.

DARK ANGEL

by

ELIZABETH ASHTON

HARLEQUIN BOOKS   TORONTO
WINNIPEG

Original hard cover editon published in 1974
by Mills & Boon Limited.

© Elizabeth Ashton 1974

SBN 373-01835-5

Harlequin edition published December, 1974

All the characters in this book have no existence outside the
imagination of the Author, and have no relation whatsoever to
anyone bearing the same name or names. They are not even
distantly inspired by any individual known or unknown to the
Author, and all the incidents are pure invention.

The Harlequin trade mark, consisting of the word
HARLEQUIN and the portrayal of a Harlequin, is registered
in the United States Patent Office and in the Canada Trade
Marks Office.

Printed in Canada
1835

CHAPTER ONE

THREE figures were climbing up a rough path between the gnarled trunks of an olive grove, two girls and a donkey. The younger girl—she was only a child—bestrode the animal's shaggy back, while her sister scrambled up the track beside her. Francesca Temple was a lissom wand of a girl, with shining pale gold hair blown by the breeze into a nimbus about her oval face, and delicate features, clear as a cameo against the dark background of the trees. The path was cut through the terraces on which the olives grew, and was so steep and stony that only a creature as sure-footed as a goat or a donkey could have negotiated it, but Francesca was as nimble as either animal.

They reached a level space, where a pile of stones indicated that some building had once been erected there, and Francesca called a halt.

'That's far enough, Stacey,' she insisted. 'Besides, isn't this the boundary of our land?'

The child pouted rebelliously. 'I wanted to go right up to the Castello, and nobody'd mind. You're lazy, Fran, living in London has made you soft.'

The other girl laughed. 'I haven't got used to the Italian sun yet, and I don't want to go up to the Castello. We might run into the Marchese, and I'm not dressed for a formal call.'

She was wearing white trousers, dustied by her climb, and a sleeveless top, not the sort of garb which would be approved by an Italian nobleman of the old school, as she knew very well, besides which the glimpses she had had of him showed him to be a rather

5

formidable personage, and though sooner or later she would have to encounter him, she would prefer to be looking her best when she did so.

Beyond their resting place, the ground continued upward to the top of the steep hill upon which the village and Castello were perched. The beige-coloured houses of Castel Vecchio were clustered round the tall narrow tower of the church, with the Castello next to it, survivors from medieval times when the community had sought the higher ground as a refuge from pirate raiders invading the coast. Today its young people were drifting away from the tall houses with their dilapidated green shutters to the busy seaside towns, and the narrow climbing streets echoed more frequently to the footfalls of curious tourists than those of its diminishing inhabitants. But few visitors had as yet disturbed its peace, and the ancient buildings drowsed in the bright spring sunshine.

The Castello, Francesca thought, looked a little grim, its battlements outlined against the blue of the sky, standing high upon its precipitous eminence, a monument commemorating the many dark deeds that its thick walls had witnessed.

She turned about and looked down the way they had come. The sunlight illuminated the shallow valley beneath them with harsh brilliance, and though it was only late spring, much of the vegetation had a burned-up appearance, except for the silver foliage of the olive trees, pewter and black on brown.

The valley was dotted with houses and bisected by narrow, winding roads, which wended into the arid foothills, first bastions of the Ligurian Apennines, the gaunt peaks of which fretted the skyline.

Directly beneath them was the roof of their home, Bellavista. Francesca Temple had come out to join her family for a holiday after completing a domestic science course in London. She had not seen them for a year, not since her grandmother with whom she had been living had died, and they were almost strangers to her. Moreover, between her and her sister, Stacey— her full name was Anastasia—there was a big gap in years. The child was only nine, the unexpected product of a final upsurge of dying fires, an inexcusable piece of carelessness, the elder Mrs Temple had declared in her forthright way, for it was becoming apparent that her son Henry, her only child, would never make a living out of Bellavista, and an increase in the family was hardly justified.

It was not wholly Henry's fault; the place was not sufficiently productive to support him, and he was only able to continue while his mother subsidised him. She had bought the place for him originally because Francesca's mother, Stella, suffered from asthma and it was thought the mild climate would be beneficial to her health. She had been very ill after Francesca's birth, and her mother-in-law had taken charge of the baby, but when Stella was better, she refused to relinquish her, finding in the child an interest for her old age. Stella had acquiesced, secretly rather glad to be relieved of maternal responsibilities, and Henry was pleased to be able to make some recompense for his mother's generosity. She was half Italian, Francesca had been named for her, and after she was widowed her heart turned towards her mother's people. She frequently visited Bellavista, but rarely took her granddaughter with her.

She spared no expense upon Francesca's education, and selected her studies with a secret project of her own in mind, with one exception. Francesca had a yen for *haute cuisine* and had insisted upon including

7

high-class cookery among her subjects.

'It's useful knowledge,' she had pointed out. 'If anything happens to you, I can always make a living at it.'

The elder Francesca had smiled indulgently.

'Nothing is going to happen to me. Learn it by all means if you wish to do so, but your fate will lead you into higher places than the kitchen.'

She often made such cryptic remarks, which Francesca let pass unheeded. She knew that her grandmother wanted her to make a good marriage, but she had her own ideas about that. Not wishing to antagonise the generous old lady, she kept them to herself. Time enough to oppose her when she came up with something definite.

Then suddenly and unexpectedly, Mrs Temple died of a stroke, and when her affairs were wound up it was discovered that contrary to expectations, she had little to leave. The bulk of her income was an annuity, and since she was addicted to gambling on the Stock Exchange, most of her investments proved to be worthless. She left Francesca a few hundreds, most of which the girl expended upon her domestic science course, and to Henry she left Bellavista with the proviso that it should come to Francesca upon his decease.

Her course completed, Francesca had come home for a vacation before seeking a post, and it had been arranged that Desmond Watson was to come out to join her as soon as he could get away.

Francesca was looking forward eagerly to his coming, for upon what happened then her future depended. Desmond and she had one of those casual, affectionate connections which often ripen into marriage. She fully intended to find a job, for she would need her earnings to save up for her wedding, and since Desmond did not earn a big salary, it might be necessary for her to continue working for a while after it. They were not yet engaged, but she hoped that their joint holiday would produce the ring. He was to visit Bellavista during his stay, and unwittingly her glamorised account of the place had given him an exaggerated picture of it, and its revenues.

Desmond had appeared upon the scene before Mrs Temple's death. Though secretly dismayed, the old lady had issued no positive veto, being wise enough to know that opposition bred defiance, but he was not the sort of man she wished her granddaughter to marry. She was convinced that beneath his facile charm the young man had no real depth of character and trusted to time and Francesca's own good sense to discover his weaknesses before it was too late. Delay being important, she had insisted that the girl was too young to consider marriage.

'But I'm twenty-one,' Francesca protested. 'Lots of girls marry at my age.'

'Does he think you'll inherit money?' Mrs Temple asked bluntly.

Francesca flared up at that. Desmond was not mercenary, she declared, he did not even know that she might have some money. Her grandmother was being prejudiced and unfair.

'Well, don't do anything in a hurry,' Mrs Temple sighed. 'I shan't last much longer, Fran, and I can't do without you.'

'Rubbish, you'll last for years yet,' Francesca returned, scorning this subtle blackmail.

But Francesca was proved wrong.

She had never analysed the depths of her feelings for Desmond. It was normal for a girl of her years to have a young man in tow. Desmond was good-looking and attractive and she fancied herself in love. That he never touched her deepest emotions did not strike her as significant. She was sure that romantic love was a thing that only existed in novels and her pleasant affectionate comradeship with him was a sufficient foundation for marriage. Possibly she was right and if events had followed the course which she expected, she might have settled down to an even tenor of tranquil days unlit by any height of ecstasy or depths of passion. Such was not to be.

Upon her arrival home, Francesca was appalled by the state of affairs at Bellavista. Stacey was running wild, though her father had taught her to read and write. The house was neglected and falling to pieces. Without his mother's subsidies, Henry could not maintain the place, and in addition, Stella was ailing.

Not being stupid, Francesca suspected it could not be long before her father would be unable to pay his commitments and the property would have to be sold. She only hoped its price would be a sufficient sum to provide an income for her parents.

Standing on the boundary between their neighbour's well-tended estate and their own neglected one, Francesca was feeling despondent. Anastasia too was dimly aware that in some way her security was threatened, but she attributed it to the wrong cause.

'I love Italy,' she announced. 'I think I should die anywhere else. Granny was always telling Daddy I ought to go to school in England. I'd hate that. I'm so glad she died and can't make me go.'

Francesca was shocked. 'You mustn't say that! We all owe a great deal to Granny and I miss her terribly.'

'But she was ever so old,' Stacey pointed out. 'She couldn't have lived much longer. I liked her all right until she tried to make Daddy send me away.'

Francesca looked at her sister critically. Wearing shorts and a tee-shirt, bare-footed, her hair tangled by the breeze, she looked a thorough little savage, and the donkey she bestrode completed the picture.

'She wanted you to be educated instead of becoming a barbarian,' Francesca told her. 'Which is what you are doing.'

Stacey leaned forward and fondled her mount's large ears.

'Who cares?' she cried rebelliously. 'I like being a barbarian.'

'You ought to go to school,' her sister persisted, wondering if and when she married Desmond, he would agree to having the child to live with them during term time. 'Perhaps I could take you to England with me when I go back.'

Stacey looked at her in surprise. 'Go back? Aren't you going to live here with us?'

'I can't, Stacey. I've got to earn a living, and I may be getting married.'

Stacey slid off the donkey, leaving it to forage among the dry vegetation.

'Who to?' she demanded.

'A boy I met in London. He's ever so nice. You'll like him.'

'No, I shan't,' Stacey said positively. 'That's torn it. I'd planned that you'd fall in love with Angelo, then you would live here always, and never have to work.'

'Angelo?' Francesca queried. 'Who's he?'

'You know—you must have heard of him, he's the Marchese's son. He's come home to the Castello.' She jerked her head towards it. 'He's so handsome, Fran, like the prince in a fairy story.'

Francesca glanced at the formidable building on top of the hill.

'Very suitable. The Castello looks like something out of a fairy story,' she agreed, laughing. 'Of course I knew the Marchese had a son, but I didn't remember his name was Angelo. I wouldn't want to marry an Italian, dear, and no doubt he's engaged already.'

'I'm sure he's not.' Stacey was emphatic. 'Rosa says he's come home to ... er ... settle down, but she doesn't think he's fixed on a wife.'

'You mustn't listen to servants' gossip,' Francesca reprimanded her, for Rosa was the girl who helped in the house. 'But you can be quite sure there's a lady if he's come home to be married.'

She had heard stories about Angelo Vittorini, the winner of last year's Grand Prix. He was the sort of dashing, picturesque personality that attracted notice everywhere. He was reputed to frequent the casinos of San Remo and Monte Carlo, where he had phenomenal luck, and to be the lover of beautiful and wealthy women, with whom he was also successful. Angelo, she thought, was a singularly inappropriate name for such an individual.

So he had been recalled by his stern father to espouse some innocent young girl to perpetuate his name, and once his duty was done, she would be mewed up in that rather sinister-looking castle, while he returned to his former gay life. Francesca felt a flash of pity for the Vittorini bride, but doubtless the girl would have been trained for such a position and would expect nothing more from her husband. How different her own union with Desmond would be, for they would be friends and comrades as well as lovers, sharing their common lot of hopes and fears, and always together.

'I'm glad I'm not Italian,' she said fervently.

'Why?' Stacey asked. 'Italians are nice.'

'Well, among the aristocracy anyway, I believe girls still have to marry the man selected for them for the sake of the family. There's generally land involved and it entails dowries and contracts, which are considered so much more important than love.'

'You won't be able to help falling in love with Angelo,' Stacey said insinuatingly. 'And I guess he'll fall for you. You're so pretty, Fran, and—and unusual somehow, like a fairy princess. I'd set my heart on you two getting married.'

Francesca laughed. 'Sorry to disappoint you, darling, but I'm not susceptible to Latin charm, and I've got my Desmond, who'll suit me a lot better, being British. As you know, I'm spending the weekend with my friends in Imperia, and I'll be bringing him back with me on Monday.'

Stacey looked disgruntled. 'Mummy and Daddy don't want him here,' she announced.

'Oh, really, why ever not?' Francesca exclaimed, thinking Stacey must have got a wrong impression. 'He wants to meet my family, and I think it's time he did.'

She could not believe that her parents would object to Desmond's visit. They had not even seen him. Possibly they did not think he was good enough for her. Henry had inherited slightly grandiose ideas from his mother, but they ought to be thankful that she had found herself a steady young man.

'Perhaps he'll call tomorrow,' Stacey remarked.

'Who, darling?'

'Angelo, of course.'

'Shouldn't you call him Signor Vittorini?' Francesca suggested.

Stacey shook her head. 'He said I could call him Angelo.'

Francesca was startled. She had had no idea that the

heir to the Castello was on such intimate terms with her family, but the explanation Stacey then offered was even more disconcerting.

'I often go to the Castello. The chef's a great pal of mine. He gives me sweets. Angelo does come home sometimes, you know, though you've always missed his visits. When I was littler, he said he'd love to have a fair-haired *bambino* like me.'

'Oh, did he?' Francesca did not like to think of her little sister hanging about the castle kitchen, though she was aware of the easy familiarity that often existed between master and servants in an Italian household. She could hardly blame her for seeking companionship wherever it was available, for the child was often lonely, since her mother had little time for her, being absorbed in her own health, and the Italians were devoted to children.

'I hope you don't ask for anything when you go there,' she told Stacey, for she did not like to think of her little sister begging.

'Of course I don't, but if Beppo, that's the chef, offers something nice, I'd be silly to say no. They have such lovely things to eat.'

The menus at Bellavista had been curtailed owing to financial stringency, and both sisters sighed.

'I expect you'll get lots of good things at your friends',' Stacey went on wistfully. 'Wish I could come too.'

These friends, the Calvis, had asked Francesca for a visit which was to include a dance to celebrate the eldest son's engagement.

'I'm sorry, darling, but it's a grown-up do.'

'Wish I was grown up, then I could marry Angelo.'

'If you were, you wouldn't want to.' Francesca was a little sharp, for this Italian Casanova seemed to have

14

bewitched her sister. 'If you were grown up, you'd see through the glamour.'

'No, I wouldn't,' Stacey insisted firmly, unwilling to admit that she did not know what glamour meant.

The Calvis' dance, in actuality a masked fancy-dress ball, was an almost unprecedented event and had been inaugurated by Giulia Calvi, the prospective bridegroom's sister, who had absorbed romantic ideas from much reading of historical novels. Suggested almost in jest, her idea had been taken up and blossomed into actuality. The Calvis were engaged in the lucrative oil business and were very well off. Like most Italians they were gay and enjoyed an excuse for fun and games.

Giulia had been a pupil with Francesca at the expensive finishing school in Switzerland to which her grandmother had sent her to complete her education, and the two girls had become friends. Giulia had been delighted to learn that Francesca would be in Italy in time to attend the great event and had insisted that she must come masked and in fancy dress.

Francesca had decided to go as Artemis, or Diana as the Romans called her, the moon goddess, and designed for herself a simple, inexpensive, but effective classical costume. Since Desmond would be in Liguria in time for the event, she had persuaded Giulia to give him an invitation.

So it was in a mood of eager anticipation that she set forth to Imperia in the small Fiat which was the family's only mode of transportation. It, like everything else on the estate, showed signs of wear and tear, and looking at it dubiously, she hoped it would get her to her destination.

Her way led up the hill and through the village, skirting the Castello and the church, descending on the further side in a series of hairpin bends, after which it passed under the autostrada, a miracle of modern engineering, to pursue an undulating course towards the coast.

Francesca had covered about half the distance, when, descending a steep declivity, the car gave a horrid lurch, and the brake refused to act. With perspiration breaking out on her brow, Francesca cut the engine and guided the vehicle on to the verge. Luckily at that point there was a verge, a ledge of rock and earth at the roadside.

Its progress checked by the dust and stones, the car came to a halt, and with a sigh of relief, Francesca sat back in her seat and considered her position.

It was still early in the afternoon, an hour when most of the inhabitants of that area rested, even though the weather was still comparatively cool. It was a dead hour, for most of the shops did not open until three o'clock and here, in the country, nothing moved on the hillsides. Moreover, the road she was on was unfrequented; she had chosen it for that reason, not liking the rash enthusiasm of Italian drivers.

A cursory examination of the car soon convinced her that only a major repair would get it going again. Possibly some vehicle would pass and give her a lift, and once arrived at the Calvis', she could ring up a garage and ask its owners to come and collect the car, when with luck it might be repaired in time for her return on the Monday morning. She sighed, thinking of the expense involved. Her father was not going to be pleased.

She got out of the car and looked about her. Long bare slopes were on either side of her, terraced, as all the cultivated land was in Liguria. Though the district was called the Riviera dei Fiori, few flowers were visible, being protected by unsightly glass and polythene.

The sun shining out of a cloudless sky was hot on her shoulders, the line of the distant sea, ultramarine in colour, was visible on the horizon. In the silence surrounding her she could hear the swish of the cars along the autostrada, but none came her way.

Surely something must pass soon, she thought despondently, and then the noise of an approaching engine rent the stillness. A car was coming fast down the hill. Francesca stepped out into the road prepared to wave it down. It appeared round the corner, a low-slung sports car, travelling at such a pace that she doubted if its driver could have noticed her signal, but apparently he had, for he pulled up some way ahead in a swirl of dust, turned in a wide arc and returned to halt beside her. She glanced at the vehicle apprehensively. It seemed to be all bonnet, and was open to the air behind the windscreen. If not actually a racing model, it was built on the same lines.

Its owner jumped out into the road, without troubling to open the low door, and came towards her. Although the day was warm, he wore a black polo-necked sweater up to his chin, his eyes were concealed by a pair of dark-tinted sunglasses, and a plume of black hair had descended upon his forehead. He was tall for an Italian, and slim built, but it was too much to hope he would prove to be British.

'I've had a breakdown,' she said. '*Un guàsto.*'

'So I see,' he returned in English, with a faint accent which betrayed that he was not a fellow-countryman. He turned his head to survey the Fiat. 'Not very surprising either. I would not call that vehicle roadworthy.'

'It's very reliable normally,' she said in its defence.

17

'We often go to Imperia in it, but this time I'm afraid it's had it.'

He took a look inside the car, moving the controls.

'*Si, signorina*, I am afraid it has,' he informed her. 'You will need a new gearbox.'

'Oh dear!' This confirmed her worst fears. 'I wonder, *signore*, if you are passing a garage, would you ask them to send someone out to attend to it?'

'Willingly, but meanwhile what will you do? Wait for them? They may be hours. In fact they may not get here until Monday morning.'

'That's true.' She was silent, mentally calculating the cost of hiring a car. The stranger was apparently studying her, with a twist of his handsome mouth, set above a square chin, the only features that she could see clearly. His critical appraisal took in her slight figure with its deceptive appearance of fragility, her large eyes, which in contrast to her pale skin and light amber hair looked like velvety pools of darkness, though actually they were a mingling of blue and grey, producing violet. Her slacks and short-sleeved shirt outlined an almost boyish figure, and in this casual garb she looked ridiculously young.

He smiled. 'Little girls like you should not be allowed out alone in old tin lizzies,' he said with a slight drawl.

She drew herself up to her full five feet four inches.

'I'm not a little girl,' she told him haughtily. 'I'm over twenty and I've driven all over these hills. It's just bad luck the Fiat should have given up today. I've a very special date.'

'Where are you making for?'

'Imperia. I'm spending the weekend with friends.'

'I also am going to Imperia. I could give you a lift.'

She looked doubtfully at the car, and noticing her

expression, he laughed.

'My latest toy, I designed her myself,' he informed her with pride. 'Ferraris made her up to my specification. She goes like a bomb.'

Francesca gave a little gasp at this information. She was unused to meeting men who could have cars constructed to their own design.

'But perhaps after I say that, you will be frightened to travel in her?' he suggested, a faint scorn in his voice. 'She is not like your little Fiat, but has many horses leashed under her bonnet.'

'I'm not in the least afraid, however many horsepower she has,' Francesca told him, not altogether truthfully. She tilted her chin at him defiantly. It was not the car that was causing her to hesitate. He was a total stranger and a foreigner. He sensed what was troubling her, and laughed again derisively.

'You imagine I may be the big, bad wolf who eats little lambs?' he asked. 'Be reassured, *signorina*, for like yourself I go upon a date, a masked ball given by the Calvis, of whom you may have heard, to celebrate young Alberto's betrothal.'

'How strange!' Francesca exclaimed. 'That's where I'm going too. I was at school with Giulia Calvi.'

'Were you really?' She had an odd sensation that her statement was no news to him. '*Bene*, that is as good as an introduction. You have, I presume, some luggage? Though there is little room to spare in my car, I daresay I can stow it somewhere.'

He dropped a caressing hand on the shining bonnet. Evidently he was very proud of his creation.

'You're being very kind.' She moved towards the Fiat to take out her suitcase. 'Won't you tell me your name?'

'No, *signorina*, that would be a pity. This is to be a

19

masked ball, and we are not supposed to disclose our identities. So I will not tell you my name nor ask for yours, though perhaps I could hazard a guess.'

Entering into the spirit of the game, she said hastily:

'Please don't, though having seen my face, I'm afraid you'll recognise me.'

'But you will be masked and I can amuse myself trying to find you.'

'That'll be a great diversion,' she returned a little tartly. His offer was an answer to her present difficulties, but with her hand on the door of the Fiat she still hesitated. The man before her had presented his credentials, so to speak, for though he had withheld his name, he had mentioned the Calvis before she had done so, but some instinct was warning her to beware. She looked searchingly at his partially concealed face, wishing he would take off his sunglasses. They were very workmanlike articles, with thick dark lenses, side-pieces, and an extra bar connecting the eye-pieces across his brow, which gave him a slightly sinister appearance, like some space age visitor from another sphere. Eyes have been described as the windows of the soul and with the possible exception of the mouth, they were a person's most revealing feature, but she was denied the sight of his. She wanted to ask him to remove the glasses, but could hardly do so on the plea that she wished to see if his eyes looked trustworthy.

So perforce she concentrated upon his mouth, but it betrayed little beyond that it was firm and well shaped, with a slightly ironical curve at the deeply indented corners, above a strong chin.

In addition, he possessed a good breadth of shoulder, a slim, supple waist and narrow hips, but that told her nothing except that his figure was elegant and athletic, a sportsman presumably, but even that was only conjecture.

Her glance dropped to his hands. They were long-fingered, brown and sinewy, fine, sensitive hands, and they looked capable. She found them reassuring. Had they been white or podgy, she would have shrunk from him.

He seemed to suspect that she was trying to sum him up, for his lips twitched into a mocking smile, but all he said was:

'Baking on this hillside is not very enjoyable. Shall we be on our way?'

It flashed across her mind that his deep, pleasant voice was that of a man, not a youth.

'Yes—well——' She turned to pull her case out of the narrow back seat. It was an old one that she had borrowed from her mother, because it was smaller than any she possessed, and as she tried to drag it through the door it caught on the handle, burst open and spilled various articles into the road.

Crimson with mortification, she started to collect them, and saw with annoyance that her companion had picked up her nightdress, a diaphanous affair in blue nylon, and was regarding it with interest. She snatched it from him, stuffed it into the top of the case, and snapped the unreliable hasps.

'It would have been more polite to look the other way,' she observed acidly.

'I only wished to assist you,' he said with amusement in his voice. 'Women's gear is no secret to me.'

'Oh, you're one of that sort?' she asked scornfully.

He shrugged his shoulders.

'I do not know what you mean by "that sort",' he returned. 'I am not in the lingerie trade, if that is what you are thinking.' She was not, and she was quite sure he knew it. 'In these days of vulgar advertising,' he went on blandly, 'all the so-called feminine mysteries are revealed in intimate detail by television. Is that not so?'

'I'm afraid it is.'

Feeling rebuked, she allowed him to take the case from her, hoping the hasps would hold, and locked the Fiat. He stowed it somewhere in the back of his vehicle, and turned to her holding out a spare pair of sunglasses.

'You had better put these on, the road reflects the glare.'

'Thank you, but I have my own.'

She fished in her handbag and came up with an ornamental pair of small blue ones.

'Inadequate,' he told her. 'Like most feminine accessories. Put these on.' They were round and dark, and would be most unbecoming.

'I'll be all right,' she demurred.

'Please to do as I say,' he ordered imperiously. 'At this rate we will never reach Imperia.'

He stepped up to her and placed the offending glasses over her eyes, and her skin crept as she felt his fingers touch the side of her head. An electric current seemed to run down her spine. With a little gasp, she said sharply:

'You are a trifle high-handed, *signore*.'

'Some women never know what is good for them,' he returned.

'Oh really!' she exclaimed. 'Well, I hope you're satisfied!' A name came into her mind, which described his slightly satanic appearance very aptly ... 'Mephistopheles!' she concluded.

He drew a quick breath which might have indicated surprise.

'Why do you call me Mephistopheles?' he asked.

'I don't know, it came into my mind, I don't know why.'

'I suspect you are a witch, for that is the character I am representing tonight, or can it be that we are *en rapport*?'

'I shouldn't think so,' she said, shying away from the intimacy this suggested. 'I'd hate to be able to read your thoughts.'

'At the moment you might find them interesting,' he observed slyly.

'I wonder. Anyway, forewarned is forearmed. Any scarlet figure will be carefully avoided tonight. I've no wish to encounter the demon tempter.'

'You should know he cannot be evaded. Allow me.' He pushed her towards his car, and as Francesca subsided on to the seat, bent to fasten the seat belt about her waist. As he leaned over her she was again aware of tingling nerves.

The car was so low that she seemed to be sitting in the road, with an acre of gleaming bonnet in front of her. Then he stepped in beside her, again disdaining to use the door, and started the engine. The car dived down the hill, the air rushing past them, the draught from the open sides blowing her hair out like a fan. The road ran in loops and curves and seemed to swoop up to meet them.

The wild ride was exhilarating. He was so close to her, for the car was narrow, that their thighs were almost touching, and she was very much aware of his lean muscular body. He drove with a fierce concentration, well knowing, as she did too, that the slightest misjudgment would send them hurtling over the precipitous incline which edged one side of the road, or smash them to pieces against the rocky bank on the other. Italian drivers, Francesca knew, always drove at top speed and most accidents were head-on collisons. He was flagrantly defying any speed limits, trusting to the road being deserted at that hour, and fortunately there was next to no traffic. Only when the solitary villas gave place to rows of houses, tall and shuttered under shallow red roofs, did he slacken speed, and began to drive almost sedately through the increasing number of vehicles.

Francesca drew a long breath of relief. She pulled off the offending sunglasses and put them under the dashboard, and taking a comb from her handbag tried to tidy her hair. Halted by traffic lights, her companion turned to look at her, and she peered at him through its tangled meshes.

'*Bene*, what did you think of her performance?' he asked.

'Oh, great, but I count myself lucky to have arrived in one piece.'

'I knew what I was doing,' he said loftily, adding appreciatively: 'You are a plucky girl, *signorina*.'

'Were you deliberately trying to test my nerves?' she asked indignantly.

'Perhaps I wanted to see what you were made of,' he returned.

'Then I hope you're satisfied,' she flashed.

The lights changed and the car moved forward.

'Very satisfied,' he told her.

Some significance in his tone caused her some inner confusion. She was only a passenger to whom he had given a lift, she assured herself. He had tried to frighten her out of sheer devilment, believing her to be a timid foreign girl, and he was merely surprised that she had not betrayed her nervousness. His was a disturbing personality, for he possessed a virile mascu-

24

linity that produced unwilling response from the female element in her. Involuntarily she tried to move further away from him, shrinking against the outer edge of the car. Desmond had never affected her so. Regarding him, if she were honest, she would have to admit that he had never given her any great thrills. She fancied that she was in love with him, not realising that she was still unaroused. Her grandmother had kept her sheltered, and during her sojourn at college she had been repelled and shocked by her colleagues' casual affairs. A romantic idealist, she thought that love should be a great adventure, culminating in the wedding night. Anticipation seemed to her to cheapen it. Desmond, ultra-modern, had thrown out hints, but she had told him frankly that she would prefer to wait. That he had agreed to do so, instead of repudiating her, as her associates had declared he would, had raised him high in her esteem and assured her that he really loved her.

Now shops and cafés lined their route which turned westward away from the harbour, from which the olive oil, source of the prosperity of Oneglia and Imperia, was exported. As they climbed yet another hill, palm trees became much in evidence, and orange and lemon trees grew in the gardens.

Before wrought iron gates set ajar, which gave access to the villa hidden from view by massed shrubs, her companion brought his car to a halt.

'With your permission, we will part here,' he said pleasantly. 'If I take you up to the house I shall have to pay my respects to the Calvis, and they will not want to be embarrassed by a visitor when they are in the midst of their preparations.'

'Quite so,' she returned a little drily, wondering if that were his real reason for not presenting himself.

With exaggerated care, he handed her her case.

'I should hate that pretty blue negligée to be again precipitated into the road,' he told her mockingly, and she could have hit him.

'Well, thanks a million,' she said coolly. 'Goodbye, *signore*.'

'Not goodbye, only *arrivederci*.'

'Of course, I shall see you tonight.'

'Certainly you will.' He smiled wickedly. 'Especially as I have a debt to collect.'

She flushed angrily. 'I know I'm under an obligation to you, but I thought you would be too generous to expect a fee,' she told him.

'I shall not ask for anything that you are unwilling to give,' he returned cryptically.

'Indeed? And what is your charge for rescuing me?'

'That you will discover in time.' He stepped back into his car, and with a wave of his hand, shot away back down the hill.

Francesca watched him go, drawing her slanted brows together. If he meant to make a pass at her during the evening he would get his face slapped, she thought irefully. Then she remembered that Desmond would be there, and though she did not consider she needed his protection, he would naturally monopolise her. This speed merchant would have no opportunity to pester her. Picking up her suitcase, she walked up to the villa.

CHAPTER TWO

ALL along the Ligurian coast the mountains come down to the sea, and the shoreline is inundated with bays, each of which contains its town or towns; they are strung along the coast like a necklace of gaudy beads. There is little level ground, and villas and hotels straggle up the slopes which are the foothills of the Ligurian Apennines. In the north, the mountains become arid and bleak, guarding the approaches to the cities of the Lombardy plain.

Imperia, capital of the province of that name, was divided into two parts, Oneglia to the east and San Maurizio to the west. It was renowned for its olive oil industry, and the prosperity this had created put its citizens among the most highly paid workers in the area. Flower-growing, the other activity, was by comparison a much more arduous existence, necessitating as it did very early rising and the watering of the plants three times a day.

The Calvis were among those who had prospered by commercial enterprise, though they were not as affluent in this respect as the Vittorinis, who practically owned the oil business. They lived in a pleasant villa on the western slopes, but their ambitious *festa* was not being held on their own premises; they had engaged accommodation in a hotel. After it was over, Francesca had been asked to return to the villa and spend the rest of her weekend with her friends, and of course Desmond was to be included in their activities.

Giulia was watching for her arrival from the first floor balcony, most of the newer houses had these embellishments, and was astonished to see Francesca walking up to the house, looking slightly dishevelled and carrying her suitcase. She ran down to meet her, exclaiming when she did so:

'*Cara mia*, what has happened? Where is the old car that rattles?'

'Somewhere in the hills between here and Bellavista,' Francesca informed her. 'And I hope your father will help me to get it collected.'

'Of course, of course, he will be most pleased to oblige you, but come in, come in, you look hot and tired, and tell me what happened. I can see that you have had an adventure.'

In the shaded *salotto* with its marble floor, over a glass of iced lemonade, Francesca related what had occurred.

Giulia was a slim, dark girl, wearing the trousers and over-blouse which was almost a uniform among the Riviera girls for daytime wear, whatever their nationality. It was Francesca's rescuer whom she found the most interesting part of her recital, and she began to speculate about his identity.

'If he drive the so peculiar car so fast, perhaps he is a racing driver,' she suggested. She spoke in English as she always did to Francesca for practice, though she used her own idiom. She ran over a list of names, concluding with: 'Camillo Ardoino, he likes the sports cars, and he lives your way, but he is short and fair, and you say this man was tall and dark. Angelo Vittorini—but no ... he uses his father's Ferrari, since he is said to have given up the sports, and I doubt if he will do us the honour of appearing tonight. Then there is Roberto—but no, I forget, he has gone to Spain. No, *cara*, I cannot imagine who it could have been, and I think that if he is here tonight, it will be proved he is one who the gate has crashed.'

'Very likely,' Francesca said, laughing. 'I'm sure he had cheek enough to do just that. But I'm dying for a bath, and my poor dress will need the iron that is hot.'

'*Si, si,* everything that we have is at your disposal.'

She led the way to Francesca's room, which had its own bathroom. 'I do not suppose that your *amico* will like that you accept this lift?' she asked. 'Two in a sports car are very intimate, are they not? But of course you will not mention it to him.'

Francesca coloured slightly, recalling her sensations when in close proximity to the stranger under discussion.

'Des won't mind,' she said quickly.

'An Italian boy would be very jealous.'

'Des isn't like that. He has every confidence in me.'

'I should not like that,' Giulia declared as she threw open the door of the tiled bathroom. 'A man should be furious if another as much as looks at his *inamorata.*'

'And I would not like that,' Francesca laughed again. 'I'd hate to think Des didn't trust me.'

'But if a man is not jealous how can a girl believe in his love?' Giulia persisted.

Francesca said vaguely that there were plenty of other ways of proving it. Giulia's attitude was typically Latin. She enjoyed the excitement of quarrels and petty intrigues, treating her own swains to a great display of feminine coquetry. She never forgot that she was a woman and could not understand the easy comradeship between British men and girls. Francesca fully intended to tell Desmond all about her little adventure and expected to have a good laugh over it.

Her dress was none the worse for its rough handling, though she had left behind the long bow that should have accompanied it on the floor of the Fiat, unwilling to burden her cavalier with such an awkward accessory. She considered it was no great loss, for though in character, it would have been a nuisance. The short white tunic was kilted round her waist, its sleeveless folds caught together with silver studs, veiling her shoulders. Slung over one of them she wore a quiver containing faked arrows and the crescent moon on a silver band round her flowing hair. Her sandals, laced to the knee, were also silver. The costume suited her, emphasising her natural aloofness, an almost fey quality which she possessed. She looked very much the virgin huntress.

Giulia was going as a Florentine lady—a choice she was rather regretting, for the heavy brocade skirts of her dress were cumbersome, though she looked very handsome and impressive with her black hair piled up under a pearl-bordered velvet cap.

'I think yours is the more sensible costume,' she said. 'It does not impede your movements.'

'But I don't look anything like as distinguished as you do,' Francesca declared. 'You look quite magnificent. With you around, no one will notice me.'

'They will,' Giulia assured her. 'You have, what you say, an appearance not quite of this world. It is very provocative, *cara*, men will be drawn to you like flies to honey. They are always attracted by the seemingly unattainable.'

'Rubbish!' Francesca energetically squashed this flight of fancy. 'You make me sound like a freak!'

Desmond Watson came to meet the Calvis' car as it drew up outside the hotel. The girls had put on their masks during the short drive. He was a well-built young man with a fresh complexion and light brown hair which he wore long. Blue-eyed, he had an ingenuous expression, which concealed a calculating mind. With an Englishman's normal dislike of dressing up, he had contented himself with hiring a black domino, beneath which he could wear his shirt and trousers. He knew Giulia, having met her previously, and he grumbled about having to wear masks, as he handed the girls out of the car. Giulia's parents had gone on ahead to make sure all was in readiness.

'Like a lot of kids playing cops and robbers,' he complained. 'And it deceives nobody. I knew you two at once.'

'I think you recognised the car,' Giulia giggled. 'And of course you recognised Fran. No mask can deceive the eyes of a lover.'

'I'd know Fran's legs anywhere,' Desmond declared, looking at them appreciatively.

'Well, I shouldn't have known you, but for your voice,' Francesca told him, 'all shrouded up in that hood and gown. You look like something out of the Inquisition.'

A comparison which seemed to please him, and he told the girls they both looked very nice, which was his stock compliment, anything more comprehensive being beyond his imagination.

They passed through a marble vestibule ornamented with potted plants, and through swing doors beyond, where an usher glanced at their invitation cards and waved them on to where Signor and Signora Calvi waited to receive their guests. They were the only people not masked. They stood under the glittering chandeliers, smiling graciously, as each new arrival came up to them, making some appropriate comment on their costume, pretending of course not to know who they were.

Doors at the further end of the long room led on to a terrace, which had access to a garden on a lower level, and they were wide open to the night.

'You see it would be quite easy to gatecrash,' Giulia murmured to Francesca, indicating them.

'Who'd want to do that?' Desmond asked, eyeing the assembled company dubiously; they were not the sort of people he usually mingled with when he was in search of recreation, for he preferred night clubs, though his work often took him to such assemblies. He was wondering if it would be permitted to write this one up for his paper.

'That's a long story,' Francesca informed him, but she had no chance to tell it, for as the orchestra struck up, he muttered:

'Well, let's get going,' and swept her into a waltz.

When they did sit down on the hard gilt chairs lining the walls, he was eager to tell her about the amusing things that he had found to do.

'It's a pity Bellavista is so off the map,' he said regretfully. 'We could have had much more fun down here.'

'But I want you to meet my parents,' she told him, thinking he ought to be more eager to do so, since they were to become engaged, but she supposed meeting future in-laws was always something of an ordeal, like being on approval. Not that her parents' approval or disapproval would influence them. They were modern young people and would brook no interference with their plans.

'And I want you to see Bellavista,' she went on. 'It's my home.'

'I've heard it's quite a profitable place.'

She nearly said it used to be, but checked herself. No need to denigrate the estate before he had even seen it, but she feared that even his inexperienced eyes would notice it was going downhill, and all that that implied.

Giulia's brother Alberto was slim and debonair in doublet and tights. He was in business in Milano and considered a good match for the dark-eyed Beatrice Murano. Both families were there in force and beaming approval on the young couple. Watching them, Desmond said:

'Italians make quite a thing of their families. Did those two have any choice in the matter?'

'It's not exactly an arranged marriage, if that's what you mean,' Francesca told him, having had all the details from Giulia. 'Alberto was introduced to Bea with that intention, and they conveniently fell in love—at least she did. Not difficult when you consider that she's been kept at a convent school and was ready to fall for the first presentable male she met. He, of course, has reached the stage when he's wanting to settle down . . .' She paused, recalling that she had heard that phrase in connection with someone else. Young Alberto, like Angelo Vittorini, had probably had his fling and was quite agreeable to accepting the young, adoring bride—and her dowry—which had been produced for him. An excellent arrangement—for the man.

'Continental marriages are very complicated affairs,' she went on, 'with contracts, settlements and dowries to be considered.'

'And do you have a dowry, sweetheart?' he asked jokingly. 'A few vines perhaps, or a fig tree?'

'Is that why you want to marry me?' she asked lightly, wondering if she had ever hinted to him that Bellavista should eventually come to her, if there was anything left, which appeared extremely unlikely.

'Don't be silly,' he said reprovingly, but behind his mask there was a speculative gleam in his eyes. 'What's the matter?' For she had given an exclamation. She had at that moment caught sight of Mephistopheles.

He had evidently only just arrived, for he was bending over Signora Calvi's hand and apparently saying something very gallant, for her handsome face was wreathed in gratified smiles. Then he straightened himself and glanced round the room. Scarlet tights, tunic, cloak, horned headdress and of course a mask made of him a barbaric and arresting figure, but the arrogant way in which he carried himself was familiar. It must be her cavalier of the road, for no one else was wearing that particular dress. Desmond's gaze followed hers, and he exclaimed,

'Good lord, look what's come!'

'The demon king,' Francesca said, giggling.

'So it seems. Only a dago could wear that get-up—and carry it off,' Desmond said grudgingly as the slim scarlet figure moved away with a long lithe stride to where a dark, forbidding-looking girl was sitting.

'He evidently knows where the money is,' Desmond went on. 'That's Maria Donizetti, I'm sure. I'd know that shape anywhere, even if her whole head was covered. One of the richest heiresses on the Riviera.'

'You've met her?'

Desmond smiled. 'Darling, she doesn't condescend to the likes of me, but she was pointed out to me. It's part of my job to know who's who. She seems acquainted with Mephisto.

For the girl had risen with alacrity and was moving off in the red demon's arms.

Francesca was vaguely disappointed, though she assured herself that she was relieved that he had not noticed her. She did not know quite what she had anticipated, possibly that he would rush up to her and claim her, which would have been awkward since she had not yet told Desmond of their encounter. She had certainly not expected to be completely ignored. A little reflection showed her that her fears, if they were fears, were groundless. He was here among his own friends—Maria Donizetti certainly appeared to be aware of his identity—rich influential people, and would have forgotten that she was to be present. He was far and away the most striking personality there, and it would have been embarrassing to be singled out by him, and presumptuous to imagine that he would do so.

She looked curiously at his partner as they went past her in the dance. Maria Donizetti wore an Eastern dress, wide transparent trousers and a sleeveless embroidered jacket over a white blouse—she had not gone so far as to bare her midriff—with a silk sash about her waist. Long black hair hung down her back under a thin veil; a black mask obscured the upper half of her face, the filmy yashmak softened but did not conceal the strong lines of her slightly underhung jaw and big nose. There were jewels on arms, neck and ankles, and a big stone sparkled on the band which encircled her brow. They were obviously real ones. Mephistopheles' mouth was curved in the slightly satirical smile which she well remembered, but he seemed wholly absorbed in his partner, who was talking volubly while they danced. Then they were lost to view on the crowded floor.

Desmond jumped to his feet.

'Come on, Fran, we've sat still long enough, though I don't care much for these old-fashioned waltzes and whatnot, they're so slow, but at least they have one advantage.' He put his arm around her. 'I can get close to you.'

Supper was a buffet meal, served in an adjoining room. Everybody was busy pretending they could not see through each other's disguises, though in most cases their friends were easily identifiable. Francesca had recognized Alberto and Beatrice at once.

Back in the ballroom, the chandeliers were dimmed and coloured spotlights flickered over the whirling couples. Paper chains were thrown by the more audacious young men, with the object of encircling various couples, who looked only too eager to be joined together.

Throughout the evening, Francesca had persistently clung to Desmond, feeling the need of his protection against that menacing scarlet figure, but as it seemed to have no intention of coming near her, she allowed herself to become separated from him in what was the equivalent of an 'excuse me' dance. After that she lost him.

The lilting music, the shaded lights produced an atmosphere of sensuous languor. At midnight the lights would go up, and the engaged couple toasted; then the dancers would discover who had been their partners during the evening, in those cases where they were still in doubt.

No one attempted familiarities in the confines of the ballroom, that would have been bad manners, and several chaperones watched closely in the endeavour to maintain guard over the unmarried girls. But frequently couples disappeared through the tall windows on to the terrace, to return surreptitiously adjusting their costumes.

Francesca danced with whoever asked her, the Chianti she had drunk at supper having gone slightly to her head. She responded to her partners' gallantries with gay repartee, avoiding being lured outside, until one enterprising young man swung her out on to the terrace before she was aware of his intention. In its shadows, he tried to make love to her, but she broke from his embrace and ran down the steps which led to the dimness of the garden, a nymph pursued by a satyr.

Since she was determined to elude him, he soon wearied of the chase, after blundering into a statue, and left her to go in search of easier prey.

Francesca remained in the garden, enjoying the cool night air. Though whispers and stifled giggles proclaimed that the place was not without tenants, there was no one in her immediate vicinity. She moved silently over the paved paths, across which cypresses threw fingers of dark shadow, and hidden roses scented the air, to the limits of its confines. Here a low stone wall separated it from a steep drop into the road below. She could see the lights of the town spread out beneath her, and the shimmer of the sea, where a waning moon was arising, an orange disc, with a bite out of its upper half. Its light was not yet strong enough obscure the stars, which formed a gilded mosaic above her head.

'So at last I have found you!'

Francesca wheeled round, fearing that her amorous partner had caught up with her, but she knew that voice, and it was not that of her erstwhile cavalier. The night turned his scarlet to black, but there was no mistaking that arrogant figure.

'I thought you were too occupied to notice me,' she returned, aware that her heartbeats had accelerated.

He leaned negligently against the plinth of one of the statues with which the garden was adorned, and drawled:

'Of course I noticed you, but you seemed engrossed in the moron in the black domino. Might one enquire who he was?'

'He's not a moron, he's my countryman, my—er——'

She hesitated, curiously reluctant to admit Desmond's claim upon her. After all, she was not yet officially engaged. 'Boy-friend,' she concluded.

She sensed a stiffening in him, as if this admission was unwelcome, but his suave tones betrayed nothing, as he asked:

'Boy-friend? What does that mean? He did not look a boy.'

'It's an English expression for a sentimental relationship,' she explained, 'that's about to ripen into something closer.' And felt rather pleased with her definition.

'Or might wither away?' he suggested.

She said nothing to that, merely shrugging her shoulders. Silence fell between them, the music from the dance filtering through to them mingling with the sound of traffic on the road below. She could feel his eyes upon her through his mask, pin-points of light like those of a snake. Nervously she put out a hand and pulled at a geranium plant beside her in a stone urn. Unable to bear his scrutiny any longer, she murmured:

'Why did you follow me? What do you want?'

He laughed gaily. 'Why, to resume our acquaintanceship and if possible increase its scope. You intrigue me, you little northern lily, and your costume is well chosen. Artemis, the virgin huntress, but even she fell for Endymion.'

He continued to study her, from her hair, pale fire in the white light, crowned by its crescent moon, to her silver-shod feet. She looked like a figure carved in alabaster, and her flesh had the translucence of that substance. Only her black mask struck a discordant note.

'A snow maiden,' he said appreciatively, 'but I wager there is fire beneath the ice.'

She was disturbed by that mesmeric gaze, which was somehow menacing because she could not see his eyes, but she was determined not to show that it affected her.

'Very hypothetical,' she retorted, with a coolness she did not feel, 'and like your former description, a load of nonsense. I must be going back.'

He disengaged himself from the plinth with a swift lithe movement, and as she tried to pass him, his hand shot out and closed over her wrist.

'Why do you want to run away?' he asked her. 'This is much more your right setting than the ballroom. You might well be the Moon Goddess come to life. You only need a couple of hounds to complete the picture. As a connoisseur of women, you please my aesthetic eye, standing there, with the rising moon behind you.' Again his glance raked her. 'Not a lily,' he murmured, 'but a more fragile blossom. The wood anemone, the windflower.'

He caught her other hand, and held it with its mate against his chest. She let them stay, unwilling to provoke him by an undignified struggle.

'Please let me go,' she besought him, with a tremor in her voice. Queer little thrills were running up her spine. This man was sexually magnetic, dangerously so, but she had no wish to become involved with him.

'Not until you have paid your debt,' he told her. 'I promised you I would come to collect it.'

Why had she not kept close to Desmond? All the evening she had been subconsciously expectant of this encounter, and it had occurred in this isolated part of the garden, from which it would be difficult to escape. There was a sort of inevitability about it that frightened her.

Then she mentally shrugged her shoulders. She was being fanciful. He was only an Italian playboy seeking an amorous diversion, and when she had paid her forfeit, that would be the last of him.

'Bit obvious, aren't you?' she said scornfully. 'Well, if you expect a kiss for helping me, I suppose I would be mean to deny you, but kisses seem to be very cheap currency here tonight.'

'They are none the less very pleasant,' he told her.

'Only when the attraction is mutual,' she returned tartly. 'Since you seem to think you've earned one, you'd better take it and free me from my obligation to you.'

'I am glad to learn that you take obligations seriously,' he remarked. 'So many women try to evade them.'

As she had expected, he released her wrists to enable him to enfold her with his arms, holding her lightly against himself, but he did not immediately avail himself of the situation. In every quivering nerve she was tensed to receive his caress, and when nothing happened, she said tautly:

'For heaven's sake get it over and done with!'

'What a charming invitation!' Slowly his arms tightened and she could feel the beat of his heart under the scarlet tunic, and feared he would notice her own was throbbing madly. But he still did not kiss her.

'I think it is for you to give,' he suggested softly, his mouth only inches from her ear.

She jerked her head back in an effort to see his shadowed face, the strengthening moonlight struck fire from the sequins ornamenting the tiny horns affixed to his headdress. Lucifer in the flesh, she thought extravagantly, but she managed to say calmly:

'That's your idea. I'm not feeling generous.'

'Obviously,' he murmured. 'I wonder why. You are British, are you not? I understand the modern English miss believes herself the equal of men and entitled to experiences once considered the masculine prerogative. You will find kissing me quite a pleasurable sensation.'

'If you imagine I belong to the permissive society, you're making a mistake,' she said with a little gasp, for his grip was squeezing her now. 'I'm not available to all and sundry, and you're hurting me.'

He relaxed his hold, but his hands moved caressingly over her shoulders and back, causing her nerves to tingle.

'Eve before the fall,' he said musingly. 'Can I not persuade you to allow me to play the part of the tempter in your paradise?'

'Very apt, since you're dressed as the devil, only in Eden he came in a serpent's guise. No, *signore*, you can't tempt me.'

'You recoil from me as something obnoxious?'

'Well, of course,' she returned untruthfully, well aware that he did not believe her. Throughout their dialogue, she had a curious feeling that he was testing her, that her reactions were important to him. That seemed unlikely, unless he was trying to ascertain if she were seduceable.

'Perhaps you are accessible to the—er—boy-friend?' he asked insinuatingly. 'You allow him to take advantage of his privileges?'

'Certainly not! He respects me, we wouldn't.... What business is it of yours?' She flung the question at him indignantly.

'*Chi lo sa?*' he murmured. 'Can it be that you are frigid?'

'What else do you expect from a snow maiden, a

41

virgin goddess and all the rest of the rigmarole?' She was becoming exasperated. 'I don't know what you're getting at with this catechism, but Desmond is a decent boy, not a wolf like you.' She moved uncomfortably in his arms. 'Look, do you want your—er—fee, or don't you? If you don't, will you kindly let me go?'

To her surprise, he dropped his arms, and as she stepped back quickly, folded them across his chest.

'I prefer to wait until you are feeling more co-operative.'

This was an anti-climax and instead of relief, she was vaguely disappointed. Ashamed of such a reaction, she said fiercely:

'You're an optimist! I shall keep out of your way in future.'

'You may be unable to avoid me.'

'Don't be absurd. You don't even know who I am.'

'I have rather more than a suspicion of your identity.'

'Indeed? Did you ask the Calvis for my name?'

'That was not necessary. Will you ask them for mine?'

She glanced at him obliquely. He was a dark shape beside her in the shadow cast by a tall cypress tree, but the moonlight caught the glitter of his eyes behind his mask, and twinkled on the sequins with which his garments were strewn. Striving to combat his undeniable fascination, she said lightly:

'No, I shan't, to me you will always be remembered as the demon king. I'm grateful for the lift you gave me, but after tonight I hope our paths do not cross again.'

He laughed. 'A vain hope. Our fates are linked.'

'I'm sure you're mistaken.'

'H'm. Are you piqued because I did not kiss you?'

'Of course not, I was relieved.' She was thankful that he could not see the blush his perspicacity had brought to her cheeks. 'If you will excuse me now, I'll leave ...'

Again he put a detaining hand on her arm.

'Are you afraid I shall tempt you from your allegiance to this—er—boy-friend? I could, you know.'

'Not vain, are you?' she asked disdainfully, again painfully aware of his touch. 'It would take more than the wiles of a practised amorist to break our understanding.'

'So that is what you think I am? But you are wrong, *amore mia*, and already you are far from indifferent to me.'

He knew very well the effect he was having upon her, and the realisation stung her.

'Please don't try to keep me, *signore*,' she said frostily. 'Desmond will think I'm lost. He'll be looking for me.'

'And you would not like him to discover you here with me? He would be incensed?'

'Oh no, he trusts me, but he would tease me.'

'Then he is very different from me. I would be furious, but then I would not have let you out of my sight.'

'The jealous Italian?'

'Precisely. I am Italian and very jealous of my woman's honour.'

'Then I presume she isn't here tonight, since you feel at liberty to seek other diversions?'

'As a matter of fact she is.'

His hand had dropped from her arm, but Francesca made no move to leave him. She was recalling the girl in the oriental dress, to whom he had gone when he first entered the room. She could not remember what Desmond had said her name was, but he had told her she was an heiress.

43

'And yet you spend your time dallying with me?' she asked reproachfully.

'Dallying? That is a word I do not know, *signorina*.'

'Well, it describes your behaviour, which since you are bespoke is most reprehensible.'

'Not at all. You see, at present she is unaware of my intentions.'

That Francesca found surprising information. From what she had seen of his dancing partner, she had looked very ready to receive his advances. She was intrigued by the relations between Mephisto and the oriental lady, and wanted to make him elucidate them.

'Your prolonged absence won't endear you to her,' she hazarded. Then remembering Giulia's attitude towards her suitors, a possible explanation of his desertion occurred to her. 'Unless you're using me to make her jealous?'

'*Signorina*, what an unworthy thought!'

'It would be in character,' she told him archly. 'Though I don't appreciate being used as a stooge.'

'That is a ridiculous assumption.' He sounded almost angry.

'Be that as it may, I really must go. *Buona notte, signore.*'

He bowed with a swirl of his cloak.

'*Arrivederci, cara mia*, because your debt is not yet paid.'

'You had your chance, but you didn't take it,' she pointed out.

'I told you I preferred to wait for your co-operation.'

'Which you will never get.'

'I am very patient, *signorina*, and very persistent.'

'I don't doubt it, but suppose you direct those qualities in the right direction, which is not towards me.'

Again he said enigmatically, '*Chi lo sa?*'

44

'But I do know. *Addio, signore.*'

She ran from him and he did not follow her, though his mocking laughter pursued her. She glanced back as she reached the steps. He was still standing in the shadow of the tree, barely distinguishable from it, and she sensed he was watching her flight. He could have meant nothing significant when he said that their fates were linked, it was only another flowery phrase, and she sincerely hoped it was not so, he was altogether too disturbing a personality with whom to conduct a flirtation.... What an idea, when her loyalty was given to Desmond! She was not a flirt anyway, and he was involved with another woman. Possibly the other one was not altogether to his taste, and it was the fortune which was the bait, and so he sought other attractions while he was still free. But he had chosen the wrong sort of girl, when he had picked upon her. Impatient with her preoccupation with him, she strove to dismiss him from her thoughts as she re-entered the ballroom.

It wanted but five minutes to midnight, and when the hour struck, the lights went up, while the motley crowd removed their masks amid coquettish giggles, exclamations of surprise or murmurs of confirmation. Few had managed to remain incognito throughout the evening. Then champagne was handed round to toast the betrothed couple.

Francesca, back with Desmond again, searched the throng with eager eyes, curious to see the uncovered face of that intriguing personality which she had twice encountered and both times veiled, but nowhere could she see a scarlet figure. Mephistopheles had disappeared.

Upon their return to the villa, she asked Giulia with carefully assumed casualness if she knew who the red devil was.

Giulia laughed. 'Since he did not turn up for the unmasking, I think it is possible he had no right to be there at all. Oh, I noticed him, everybody did, but he obviously dare not reveal his face when we unmasked. Unfortunately we do sometimes get undesirable characters sneaking into these gala affairs, or maybe he was a reporter in disguise. They have the cheek of the devil —so right, since that was what he impersonated.'

'But he seemed to know the oriental lady, Maria something or other.'

'Maria Donizetti? Poor soul, she is very plain, and would respond to any man's advances, whoever he was,' Giulia declared smugly. 'She may even have connived at his appearance here tonight.' She looked at Francesca anxiously. 'He did not make himself objectionable to you, I hope? But of course you were with Desmond all the time.'

'He was rather a striking figure, and I just wondered,' Francesca said vaguely.

She had not been with Desmond all the time, and it was plausible that Mephistopheles would impudently gatecrash if he were so inclined. She had accepted him because he had said in the first place that he knew the Calvis and was going to their dance, but everybody knew the Calvis and the *festa* had been a much-talked-about event, so that proved nothing. He had merely made a shot at random to gain her confidence. He was nothing but an adventurer, pushing his luck among the Riviera heiresses. He might even have imagined she had money too. Feeling that she had been taken for a ride, both literally and figuratively, she firmly resolved to give him no further thought.

CHAPTER THREE

On the Monday morning, with Desmond beside her, Francesca drove the repaired Fiat back into the hills. The size of the garage bill had been a shock, but she had settled it out of her own small capital, expecting that her father would refund it. More disquieting still was a warning that she could not expect the car to last much longer, though she supposed the family must be aware of its condition.

She had spent most of the previous day with Desmond, exploring the town and bathing on the beach. The Calvis had invited him to dine with them.

In the privacy of her bedroom Giulia, with the frankness of an old friend, had told Francesca that she found him a little disappointing.

'He is so ordinary, *cara mia*. He would never make my heart beat, and he has not even much wealth to recommend him.'

'I wouldn't marry for money,' Francesca had told her, smiling, 'and I don't know that I want my heart to perform gymnastics. Ours is a comfortable, friendly relationship, Giulia, we know exactly where we are with each other.'

Not like that disturbing creature whom she had met the night before, but she did not want to recall either of her encounters with Mephistopheles. He was the sort of man of whom a respectable girl should be wary.

'How dull!' was Giulia's comment.

Yet as she drove back along the road down which she had made that wild descent with him, involuntarily he was brought back into her mind. She glanced

47

surreptitiously at Desmond, sitting beside her. Though not striking, he was a personable young man, and looked attractive in his blue shirt, open at the neck, showing his sunburnt throat, but he aroused no great emotional response within her. What had the other man got that he had not? She checked her thoughts. Whatever it was, it was not an estimable quality, and he unscrupulously used it to captivate every pretty girl he met.

Pretty? She said to Desmond: 'Do you think I'm pretty?'

He broke off from some incident he was relating and gaped at her.

'What a question!'

'But do you?'

'My dear, you don't need me to tell you that. As girls go, you're hard to beat. But why this sudden demand for compliments?'

'I don't want compliments, only the truth. I was wondering how I might strike a stranger, someone who had met me for the first time.'

He turned in his seat to appraise her, the fall of her fair hair, so pale as to be almost silver, the delicacy of her features, straight nose and rounded chin, the curl of dark eyelashes above eyes which looked dark also, but which he knew in reality were a mixture of blue and hazel to be almost violet.

'Someone you met at the dance?' he asked suspiciously.

'Oh, no one in particular.' With an effort she kept her voice cool and casual. 'And in any case, we were masked.'

'A very poor disguise,' he remarked contemptuously. His eyes narrowed shrewdly. 'Are you afraid someone who was attracted by you masked might be disappointed by the reality?'

'No, of course not,' she said hastily, 'and we all unmasked at midnight.' But the Demon King had not been there when that occurred. Then she recollected that he had seen her earlier on, windblown and dusty, not at her best.... Bother the man, why did she keep thinking about him? Because he was so certain they would meet again? But he did not know where she lived, and if he sought her in Imperia, he would not find her there. Aware that Desmond was watching her curiously, she changed the subject, pointing out the terraces of olive trees which covered the hills. The terracing, the only way of retaining moisture and soil on those steep slopes, was very old. Some said it dated from Roman times.

Francesca had met Desmond at an art exhibition, showing the work of a rising artist. She was at that time taking a cursory interest in painting and she had gone alone because Mrs Temple loathed modern art. Desmond had gone because he had been designated to give the artist a write-up. He had been attracted at once by the distinguished-looking girl, whose appearance was such a contrast to the sloppily dressed art students, and, the attendance being small, had made an excuse to speak to her. From that moment the rather dull morning sparkled for both of them and they had vied with each other in deriding the incomprehensible pictures presented to them as work of genius—not of course in anyone else's hearing who might have reported their ribaldry. He ended by inviting her to lunch with him.

After that they met frequently, in spite of Mrs Temple's disapproval. Francesca was lonely and starved for young companionship. He, though captivated by her, had also an eye on the main chance. The

49

grandmother was apparently a wealthy woman, and Desmond liked the good things of life, which were often beyond his reach. When Mrs Temple died, he was astounded by Francesca's decision to take a domestic science course, for he imagined the old lady must have left her comfortably off. When gradually he came to realise that that was not so, his thoughts turned to the property in Italy. If Francesca had no fortune, she still belonged where money was. Since it never entered her head to discuss her prospects with him, he remained vague as to her exact circumstances. She had talked about looking for a job, but he attributed that to a praiseworthy desire to prove that she could earn her living, not that it was a necessity. He was very fond of her, but with his moderate means and expensive tastes, he wanted a wife with money of her own. Thus though he had hinted, he had not yet come out with a concrete proposal, he was waiting to find out what was the position at Bellavista.

As they reached the top of the steep incline, and the road skirted the Castello, Desmond looked up at the formidable pile of masonry.

'I suppose that's the castle which is responsible for the name of the village, Castel Vecchio,' he remarked. 'Must say it's imposing.'

'Yes, it's often referred to locally as Castel Diavolo, because the owners in bygone days had a somewhat lurid reputation.'

'And are the present ones any better?'

'Of course, they've become civilised. Like most of the Italian aristocracy, the Vittorinis are a very old family, going back to the year dot. The present Marchese's wife—he's a widower now—was descended from the Visconti Dukes of Milan, so Granny said, and they were a sinister lot in the fourteenth century, with their betrayals and their poisonings.'

'H'm, that castle could be the scene of a few murders, it's fantastic enough, and does the, what you call him, Marchese, indulge in similar amusements?'

'Don't be absurd, he's a respectable business man, and he's dropped the title, but his dependents around here still persist in using it.'

'What business?'

'Oil. You saw the olive oil factory at Oneglia.'

'Oh, and he buys your olives?'

'I believe so, when we've any to sell.'

They had passed through the village and were going down hill. Francesca turned the car into the narrow approach to Bellavista, and saw another car coming towards them from the house. It was a Ferrari Dino, and Desmond gave an exclamation of admiration and envy. There was not room for both cars to pass, and they came to a halt. Reluctantly, being the smaller vehicle, Francesca reversed on to the dusty verge. The other car edged carefully past them. The man at the wheel had a hawk's face, beetling brows over dark eyes, his grizzled hair still plentiful, his mouth a thin line closed like a trap. He lifted a hand and bowed in acknowledgment as he drew abreast, shooting a keen, almost malignant glance at Desmond.

'Speak of the devil,' Francesca murmured when he had gone.

'You mean that was your Marchese?'

'Yes, he must have been to see Dad. I wonder what about.'

'You'll soon find out.'

'I shall, shan't I?' But it was unlike their august neighbour to pay morning calls upon the Temples, and she shivered, involuntarily, assailed by an inexplicable presage of foreboding.

Bellavista was a square white house, with a red roof and green slatted shutters, which, in hot weather were used to cover the doors and windows. There was a stone terrace in front of it, shaded by a couple of dusty-looking palms, on which Henry Temple and his wife Stella were seated in cane chairs. Francesca brought the Fiat to a standstill in the drive below it, jumped out and taking Desmond by the hand, led him towards her parents.

Henry Temple was a slim small man, with his daughter's delicacy of feature, his thin scanty hair carefully arranged to disguise his balding scalp. Stella had the remains of great beauty, faded now, with the same dark violet eyes as Francesca. She looked, and was, delicate.

As Francesca presented Desmond, they greeted him politely, but with a faint air of hostility. She thought they did not approve of him and felt a surge of protectiveness towards him. There could be no real reason for their disapproval, except his long hair, a fashion she knew her father disliked.

'How nice of you to come,' Stella said, offering him a flaccid hand without rising from her chair. 'We so rarely have visitors. Hal, pour Mr Watson a drink.'

'Our own vintage,' Henry said, picking up the bottle on the table beside him. 'It's quite drinkable,' noticing Desmond's doubtful glance, while Francesca exclaimed:

'You must call him Desmond, he's a very great friend of mine,' putting extra warmth into her voice to cover the coolness of their reception.

A glance passed between her parents which was definitely one of dismay. Feeling incensed, Francesca went to find one of the men to carry in their cases. How dared they question her choice, she thought angrily; they were so old-fashioned. Unless she could prevent it, her father would be asking Desmond what his intentions were, and his means. Perhaps she had made a mistake in bringing him here before they were actually engaged, but that would be soon remedied. It was the outcome she was expecting from Desmond's visit.

She came back to find they were discussing Signor Vittorini, who, her father announced, had been to see him on business.

'Such a charming man, and so distinguished,' Stella gushed. 'No wonder your grandmother was so fond of him. He—he always kisses my hand.' She looked wonderingly at her small white fingers as if she could still see the Marchese's salute imprinted on them.

Henry was looking grim. 'He's only charming when he wants something.'

'Oh, what did he want?' Francesca asked anxiously.

'We won't discuss it now,' Henry said evasively, glancing at Desmond.

'But you'll have . . .' Stella began.

'All in good time,' he cut her short, and went on to ask how the dance had gone. Francesca plunged into a bright account of her doings, seconded by Desmond, at the conclusion of which she said hesitantly:

'Unfortunately the car broke down.'

He frowned at the Fiat parked before him. 'But it got you home?'

'Luckily I was able to get it repaired.'

She saw the swift look of anxiety in his eyes, and knew he was thinking of the cost, but he said nothing since a guest was present. Stella embarked upon a series of roundabout probing questions, angling to discover Desmond's status. He, quite aware of her purpose, told her bluntly:

'I'm a journalist, and I don't usually holiday

abroad, but I made an effort to be with Fran, and I wanted to meet you.'

He looked at her significantly.

'I'm sure we're very glad to do so,' she said vaguely.

'And Fran wanted to show me her home. It's a nice place,' he looked about him appreciatively. 'Must be a wonderful life here in the sun and being one's own master.'

'A dog's life,' Henry declared morosely. 'Skimping and saving trying to keep going.'

'But you own your home and land,' Desmond said insinuatingly.

Francesca caught the calculating look in his eye and the disagreeable thought occurred to her that he was assessing the value of the property, and her own interest in it. She broke in hastily:

'Any sort of cultivating is so uncertain. It's much better to have a steady job.'

He gave her an odd look, and at that moment Stacey came running in causing a diversion.

'So you're Fran's friend,' she said after she had been introduced, with such obvious disappointment that Francesca could have slapped her. She supposed that compared with the more flamboyant Italian types with which she was surrounded, he must seem a little colourless to the child, but with the problem of Stacey's future in the balance, she had hoped that she would take to him.

Desmond regarded the little girl's dusty and dishevelled appearance with disfavour, and told her coolly;

'I am, and I hope soon to be something more.'

'Oh!' Stacey ejaculated blankly, and again Francesca wanted to slap her.

Rosa brought lunch out to them on the terrace—ravioli, which she made very well, followed by some unidentifiable fish, served with fresh lettuce, concluding with slices of cheese.

'Liguria is one of the few regions in Italy without any locally made cheeses,' Henry told them. 'In fact since there are only a very few cows in this area, dairy produce is scarce.'

Desmond, who disliked Italian food, was looking a little grim.

The meal concluded, the older Temples retired for a siesta, a habit they had acquired since living in the south. Stacey departed to attend to her beloved donkey, while Francesca took Desmond for a walk to show him the extent of the estate. There was besides the olive groves, a patch of vegetables on the only piece of level ground, which had to be watered daily.

'And water is terribly expensive here,' Francesca told him with a sigh, 'but we catch a lot of rain in that tank in the winter.' She indicated a large circular concrete cistern. 'But it all has to be done by hand and we have to employ a man to do it. Daddy is too frail.'

There was also a vineyard, but the vines looked dusty and neglected compared with those on the Vittorini lands which adjoined it.

'It was all one once,' Francesca went on, looking up towards the Castello. 'They owned the whole valley. I daresay if Daddy has to sell, the Marchese would like to buy Bellavista.'

'But surely he won't have to do that?' Desmond asked anxiously.

'He's getting old and he can't afford a lot of labour. The climate suits Mummy, and for her sake he'll stay as long as he can.' She sighed again. She was uneasy about their future.

'Well, that's their affair,' Desmond said indifferently. 'They can't expect you to do anything. You've your own life to lead.' He looked at her meaningly. 'Our life,' he said softly.

But he was wondering how much the sale of Bellavista would fetch.

'Oh, well, perhaps things aren't as bad as they seem,' Francesca said hopefully.

They dined upon a chicken off the estate, Rosa assisting Francesca to prepare the meal, which required their combined skill to disguise its antiquity. Francesca discovered in the pantry a large basket of fruit, including luscious strawberries.

'Where did that come from?'

'Il Signore Marchese bring him,' Rosa informed her.

'Then why didn't we have some at lunch?' Francesca asked.

Rosa shrugged; she had had no orders to serve it.

Francesca was not going to bypass such bounty, though he surmised that the Marchese's visit had somehow displeased her father. Dinner was concluded with the strawberries, and though Henry raised his brows when he heard whence they came, he said nothing, while Stella remarked:

'It would be a pity to let such lovely fruit rot.'

'Exactly what I thought,' Francesca agreed. 'Even if there is a feud between us and the Castello.' She looked questioningly at her father.

'Perhaps they're poisoned?' Desmond suggested facetiously.

Stacey muttered, 'I wish they were,' while she stared venomously at him, and Francesca hastily changed the subject.

When they had finished, Henry said pompously:

'If your young man can spare you, I would like a few words with you, Fran. I've something to say to you.'

Mellowed by food and wine, Desmond declared that

56

he would endeavour to do without her company for a short while, and his eyes followed them inquisitively, as Francesca went with him out of the room.

He led her into the little room he called his study, in which he kept his account books and records. It contained little else, besides a shabby old desk. Francesca sat down on one of the two high chairs and presented him with the garage bill.

'I'm afraid it's rather a lot,' she said apologetically, 'but we have to keep the car running, don't we, as it's our only way of getting about.'

He looked at the amount and groaned. 'I can't pay you back, Fran. I guess this is about the last straw.'

'Are things really so bad?'

He covered his face with his hands. 'I'm finished, Fran. I can't go on. I've no money to pay my taxes and the place is heavily mortgaged. If they foreclose it'll be the end of Bellavista.'

'Oh, Daddy!' She looked appalled at his bowed figure. He seemed to have shrunk. 'Will there be nothing?'

'I might manage to pay our fares back to England, I'm due for a pension soon, but the climate there will kill your mother.'

'I'll help, of course, I can get a job as a cook, they're very well paid.'

'You'll need a mighty big salary to keep us all,' he told her kindly, 'but there is a much easier way....' He looked at her eagerly. 'If you really want to help us, that is, but it will mean a sacrifice on your part.'

She said earnestly: 'Daddy dear, you know I'll do anything I can.'

'Would you?' His eyes wandered round the shabby little room. 'It'll be a wrench to leave this place—it's been home.'

'Yes, but what is it you want me to do?'

His eyes came back to her. 'How serious is it between you and that boy?'

'Desmond? He wants me to marry him,' she said uncertainly. 'I ... we ... we're nearly engaged, but he'd wait ...' She broke off wondering if Desmond would, for if she had to help support her family, it might be a long time before they could get married. She felt a surge of rebellion; her parents had had their life, and if they had been improvident, it was their fault and not fair that they should spoil hers. They had not even brought her up, having turned her over to her grandmother, but she was moved by the despair in her father's face.

'I shall have to talk it over with him,' she told him. 'Perhaps he can suggest some solution.'

'I would rather you didn't.' Pride sharpened Henry's voice.

'But I must. This concerns him as well as me. Surely you'll have something?' she finished on a note of exasperation.

Henry sighed. 'Precious little, nor do I think you'll find that young man sympathetic. I fancy he imagines you're an heiress.'

'Daddy, don't be so unfair! I'm sure he's no such idea.'

Henry began to drum his fingers on the desk. 'There is another way out,' he said hesitantly. 'And I hoped you'd agree to it, until you produced that young man.'

'What difference does he make?'

'All the difference, if you've lost your heart to him.'

'Suppose you leave my heart out of it and tell me what you have in mind.'

'You know, or perhaps you don't know, that Signor Vittorini has always wanted Bellavista back again. My mother bought it from his brother, now deceased, it was his patrimony, but it's set right in the middle of the Vittorini estate, and the Marchese desires to make it one again.'

'You means he wants to buy it? Then if the mortgagers foreclose it will be for sale, won't it?'

'Yes, and he can probably get it dirt cheap, but he doesn't know it's mortgaged. He thinks I can hold on indefinitely. So he's suggested a way in which both properties can be amalgamated.'

'So that's what he came to see you about?'

'Yes, and he made me a definite proposition.'

'But how does this affect me?'

'He made a very generous offer. He'll pay my debts —more, he will allow us to continue to live in the house—on a condition.'

Francesca drew a long breath of relief. 'That's splendid,' she said thankfully. 'Of course you'll agree to any conditions. I suppose he wants to start cultivating the land—you wouldn't mind just being sort of caretakers, would you?' Something in her father's intent gaze caused her to falter. 'Would you?' she repeated weakly.

'No, but the condition concerns you.'

'Me?'

'Under the terms of your grandmother's will, Bellavista eventually comes to you, if there's anything left of it. He considers it would be a—er—convenient family arrangement if—er—a marriage was contracted between you and his son.'

'But I'm not free! There's Desmond.'

'You aren't officially engaged, are you, or don't you bother to get engaged nowadays?'

Francesca stared at him blankly. Her first protest had been her instinctive reaction before the full impact of his words had struck her. Now they did.

59

'But ... but ... it's medieval!' she cried. 'An arranged marriage between two people who are strangers to each other, just so that he can be sure of a property and you of a home. It's impossible, absurd. I wouldn't think of it!'

'I was afraid you'd say that.'

Silence fell between them, while Francesca licked her dry lips and looked compassionately at her father's bowed figure. She knew that she had quenched his last hope, but how could she possibly for one second consider such a preposterous suggestion?

'I haven't even met this young man,' she said quietly.

'He's always been abroad when you came here,' Henry told her. 'He's been a great traveller, but he's home now. I wonder you haven't run across him in Imperia—he's often there, and not exactly inconspicuous.'

A tiny flicker of apprehension crossed her mind. Could he possibly be...? But no. The Marchese's son drove a Ferrari Dino and would never need to gate-crash a dance at the Calvis'. They would have fallen over themselves to welcome such an illustrious guest.

'I haven't,' she said flatly, 'and really, Daddy, you must be mad to imagine for one moment that I would fall in with such a scheme.'

'It would be a remarkably good match for you,' Henry pointed out, 'the Vittorinis are an aristocratic family and wealthy. That young man you brought here today can't offer you much. Besides, it would solve all our problems. The English climate was always fatal for your mother,' his voice quivered. 'And there's Stacey—the Marchese would arrange for her future, see she was educated. He's fond of her, and she looks upon the Castello as her second home. You ... you're being selfish, Fran, but it was too much to hope that you'd be moved by the plight of your parents.' He turned away biting his lips.

'But you're being dishonest, Daddy,' Francesca said gently. 'You're deliberately concealing from the Marchese that the place will have to be sold and he can obtain it without involving his son. That, apart from the emotional blackmail you're trying to impose upon me, puts the whole proposition out of court.'

'I don't think the Marchese would mind much about that,' Henry told her surprisingly. 'You see, it isn't a new idea, your grandmother suggested it years ago. They were very thick at one time. You know she was half Italian herself, in fact I believe we share a common ancestor with them. She always intended you to marry Angelo Vittorini.'

'Granny did?' Francesca stared at him in astonishment.

'Oh yes, she had you educated for that position, except,' he smiled wryly, 'the cooking, though that might be useful knowledge for the chatelaine of a *castello*.'

Francesca began to review the past. She knew her grandmother had always wanted her to make a good match, and had been disconcerted when she had taken up with Desmond. She had not know that she had had an actual candidate in view. But surely Angelo Vittorini of all people with his notorious reputation could not have been her choice, unless she was so blinded by her regard for the father, she could not assess the son.

'From what I've heard, this Angelo is a rake and a womaniser,' she said disdainfully.

'You shouldn't believe all you hear,' her father rebuked her. 'People in the limelight are always gossiped about. He's a very charming man. Won't you at least meet him?'

Francesca laughed scornfully. 'Are you hoping he'll bewitch me? It's too late, Daddy, I've found my man. I'll do anything I can to help, except sell myself to help you out of your difficulties.'

'Women often sell themselves, as you put it, to gain a wealthy husband, and you're being offered one.' He looked at her pleadingly. 'Won't you consider it, for your mother's sake? For Stacey?'

Francesca winced. There was no other way to keep Stella in Italy, and to provide for Stacey would be a drain upon her own resources, but she could not seriously contemplate the alternative.

'It's my life we're discussing, Daddy,' she reminded him. 'I've a right to choose who I'll spend it with.'

Henry nodded mutely. Though he had not really expected that she would comply, the final defeat of all hope had crushed him. Francesca's heart smote her as she left him, but what he wanted her to do was quite impossible.

Moonlight was turning the olive trees to pewter, and softening the stark summits of the distant mountains, while the scent of roses perfumed the air, when, after this harrowing interview, Francesca asked Desmond to come outside with her.

He came with alacrity, and once out of sight of the house, he kissed her very thoroughly. She submitted, and that was the right word, for try as she would she could not wake in herself any real response. She supposed she was too preoccupied with her worries to be able to do so.

Half annoyed, half amused, Desmond released her.

'You're an icicle, darling, couldn't you do better than that?'

'Sorry, Des, but the truth is I've had a bit of a shock.' She told him all that her father had said. So absorbed was she in the telling of her story, she did not notice Desmond's consternation.

'Of course I couldn't consider such an alliance for one moment,' she concluded vehemently. 'But I'm terribly worried about my family's future.'

'Surely it's up to them to take care of it?' he asked indifferently. 'They can't expect you to do anything. Can't they get public assistance or something?'

'I ... I wouldn't know, it sounds awful.' She looked at him appealingly. 'I shall have to find work as soon as possible to help out.'

He looked startled. 'I never believed you were serious about taking a job.'

'Why not? I've had it easy too long,' she said gallantly.

He was trying to assimilate her changed position. 'This has been a blow to me too,' he announced, adding to her look of surprise, 'I mean, darling, I thought your future was secure. A beautiful home,' he glanced about him appreciatively, 'which would have made us an ideal holiday retreat, and now you tell me your father is on the verge of bankruptcy.'

She searched his face anxiously. He looked like a small boy deprived of a treat. Smitten by a sudden doubt, she enquired:

'Did my—er—expectations have any influence upon your feelings towards me, Des?'

He looked a little shamefaced. 'Of course not,' he mumbled. 'But in this country girls usually have a bit of something, and it would have been very useful. You see, I don't earn an awful lot, but instead it seems you're going to have your family on your back for God knows how long.'

'I can't leave them in the lurch, can I?'

He had nothing to say to that.

'If we combine our resources,' she went on, 'we can get some sort of a home together, and something must be done about Stacey, she's growing up a little savage.'

'But, Fran,' he exclaimed aghast, 'all this is going to take a hell of a long time. I thought—I hoped we'd be able to get married, but I'm not in a position to support you and your family.'

It was out, the proposal which she was expecting so eagerly, but since the change in her circumstances, all thought of marriage must lie in abeyance until she could see her way more clearly.

'Of course you couldn't,' she told him. 'I wouldn't expect it. I suppose they'll get themselves fixed up somehow, but in the meantime we'll just have to be patient.'

'I'm sick of waiting,' he said angrily. The moonlight, the scent of the flowers, the girl by his side, so desirable but so unattainable, were affecting his nerves. 'If you weren't such a little prude, there'd be no need. Sometimes I doubt if you really love me.'

'Love's more than mere physical gratification,' she said firmly. They had had this argument before. Desmond, she foresaw, was going to be difficult. But he was disappointed by the indefinite postponement of any possibility of marriage. It was hard upon him, but it was also a test. If his feelings for her were genuine, he would sustain her now.

'Maybe, but I'm not with your high-falutin' notions, Fran. I want the girl I love, now, not in some distant future when you've worn yourself to a frazzle trying to cope with that tiresome family of yours.' He put his arm about her coaxingly. 'Why not, Fran? You needn't be so scrupulous—everyone does it nowadays, it's nothing.'

'That's just it,' she cried. 'You cheapen it, make it

nothing. Des, don't bother me. I'm upset, and I need your comfort and help.'

'You'd find those much more satisfactory in my arms,' he told her gruffly. 'Come on, Fran, you can't expect me to wait all my life for you, which, if you have your way, I look like doing; we're only young once, you know.' He lowered his voice, speaking softly: 'A night like this is created for love and all the world's asleep except us two.' His arm tightened. 'Come with me to my room.'

'No!' She fought to free herself from his hold.

His fair face grew ugly as a reason for her reluctance occurred to him, and he said bitterly:

'Are you keeping yourself for this dago type who's ready to help you at a price? He won't expect a virgin, you may be sure. They're as rare as unicorns and nearly as big freaks. So if you must sell yourself to him, why not have your fun first?'

'Des!' The coarseness of this speech revolted her. 'I've told you I've no intention of marrying him.'

'Then perhaps you're being foolish—it's the easy way out,' he told her harshly.

'But not one I'm prepared to take—besides, I love you.'

'Then you've a funny way of showing it. Oh, Fran, Fran, I want you so!' He caught her to him, frustration causing him to be rough. 'I would willingly give you a wedding ring,' he said against her ear, 'but I'm not prepared to wait for ever. It's now or never, Fran. Please, please!'

Preoccupied with each other, neither noticed the car which had stopped at a little distance from them, nor the man who had slid from the driver's seat. Screened by a luxuriant fig tree, he was watching and listening with wry amusement. Only as Desmond bent Francesca backwards in his arms, he uttered an imprecation and strode towards them. But Francesca, summoning all her strength, drove her fist into Desmond's hungry mouth, and twisting free from him, ran for the shelter of the house.

Desmond did not pursue her. He stood fingering his lips gingerly, for Francesca's blow had been a hard one, relieving his feelings in a flood of sultry language. The newcomer approached him.

'Perhaps, *signore*, after that setback, you would like a drive back to the town?' he enquired in a sauve, silky tone. 'My car is at your service.'

Desmond was muttering, 'Damn all women!'

'*D'accordo*,' the other man agreed. 'May I drive you to the coast?'

Desmond became aware of the stranger's dark, menacing presence, and stared at him blankly. 'Who the devil are you, and where did you spring from?'

'I happened to be passing, and stopped because the lady seemed to need assistance, but she was well able to defend herself. As for who I am,' he drew himself up proudly, 'I am someone who has considerable influence around here, and I suggest it might be more healthy for you to leave the vicinity.'

'I'm not going at your bidding,' Desmond said truculently.

'Ah, but perhaps I can persuade you to change your mind.'

The two men conversed for some moments, then the stranger went back to his car, and Desmond hastened towards the house, throwing uneasy glances from side to side as if he expected every bush concealed an assassin.

Lying on her bed, Francesca was reviewing the past

scene. Just why she had repulsed Desmond so violently she was not sure, except that his suggestion had roused an intense recoil. After all, according to modern standards, his demands were justifiable, but hitherto he had always respected her fastidiousness. The influence of the southern night might be to blame, causing him to lose his head. Cool herself, she had not realised that she might be putting a strain upon him by her denial, but she was confident that in the morning he would have recovered himself and be full of apologies. She was confident that once he had thought over the situation he would be ready to help her with her plans. The disclosure of her real position had come as a disappointment to him, but she was too loyal to suspect that he had had any mercenary motives regarding her. After all he had mentioned marriage after she had told him she had no prospects, and it was only the long delay which seemed unavoidable, that had upset him.

She heard the creak of the front door opening and light footsteps along the passage. He was going to his room. All the rooms at Bella Vista were on one level, with windows opening on to the terrace. Only the kitchens and the garage were below it. Compunction struck her. Poor Desmond, he had had a raw deal. Almost she was ready to go to him and affect a reconciliation, almost but not quite, for she knew how it would end. But did it really matter? He was her man, soon to be her acknowledged fiancé; was it possible that she was really so cold and old-fashioned? She got out of bed and put on her dressing-gown and slippers, standing hesitating in the middle of the room. She heard footsteps again, outside on the terrace, running down the steps, and the scrape of feet on the gravel below it. He must have gone outside again, unable to sleep. That decided her. She would join him in the garden, express her contrition and make her surrender. She went to the window, and pushed it ajar, and halted, startled, as she heard the sound of a car starting up. Desmond was going, he could not forgive her rebuff, but he must have taken the Fiat to make his getaway, and that was a piece of effrontery difficult to forgive. She flung the window wide and stepped on to the terrace. The black shape of a big car was quietly negotiating the track leading on to the road. Definitely not the Fiat, which could not traverse its rough surface without snorts and bangs. A taxi? But Desmond could not have summoned one, since the telephone was disconnected.

Mystified, she moved down the terrace to his room and found his window ajar. Stepping inside and switching on the light, she saw that all his things were gone and propped on the dressing-table was a note addressed to herself. She tore it open with impatient fingers. He asked her to make his apologies to her people, he had been forced to go—the word forced was heavily underscored. He was pained to discover that she had been two-timing him, but if she had a change of heart, she knew where to find him. He signed himself, 'Your loving and disappointed Des.'

Francesca turned the scribbled note this way and that, trying to discover some hidden meaning. What could have happened to make him doubt her, unless it was an attempt to excuse his desertion? He knew very well that she did not want the Italian, and what could have forced him to leave?

Puzzled, she went back to her own room, mulling over Desmond's flight. Had she offended him beyond forgiveness? But it was uncharacteristic of him to go away; normally after a tiff, he would wait until the next morning when he would have expressed his grievances forcibly and expected her contrition. Was it her changed circumstances that had scared him? She could not accept that, Desmond could not be such a poor creature. She was assailed by a dreadful feeling of desertion; she had thought that he would be her prop and her anchor in her dilemma. Faults he had in plenty—who had not?—but she could not believe that he had failed her. But the evidence of his empty room, his note, and the disappearing car was incontestable. Desmond had run away and left her in the lurch.

CHAPTER FOUR

FRANCESCA rose early next morning, heavy-eyed after a restless night. She felt flat and drained, all the eager anticipation with which she had come to Bellavista finally extinguished by Desmond's desertion.

Coffee and rolls awaited her on the terrace, which was pleasantly cool at that hour. Stella always breakfasted in bed, and Henry had not returned from his morning inspection of his domain, but Stacey was present hungrily devouring her rolls and jam, butter being a luxury they could not often afford.

Francesca studied her young sister thoughtfully. Stacey showed promise of being beautiful; she had the same delicacy of feature as her mother and sister, the same violet eyes, and her limbs, as she sprawled in her chair had the careless grace of a young feline. Added to her physical attributes, she showed indications of a lively intelligence, and a capacity for affection, coupled with a rebellious independence. Francesca sighed thinking that without firm guidance the child was heading for disaster.

Stacey stared at her sister reproachfully as she sat down

'Daddy says you don't care what becomes of us,' she announced. 'And I'll have to go to England and to school with a lot of horrid boys and girls who'll tease me for being ignorant. But I won't go, I'll run away first, but then I'd have to leave Bruno.' Bruno was her donkey's name. 'What'll happen to him?' she wailed, while her eyes filled with tears. 'I couldn't bear for him to be ill-treated.'

'We'll find him a good home,' Francesca said sooth-
ingly, pouring out a cup of coffee. Bruno was the least
of her problems.

'Where is he?' Stacey demanded suddenly. 'Rosa
says he's not in his room.' She was referring to Desmond. Francesca told her painfully:

'He had to leave.' And she wondered what excuse
she could invent for the young man's precipitate departure.

'You've quarrelled!' the child declared trium-
phantly. 'Now you'll marry Angelo and we can stay
here and I can keep Bruno.'

Francesca thought her father might have refrained
from discussing her affairs with the child, as he appeared to have done, but perhaps he hoped that Stacey
might influence her. She said gently:

'It isn't as simple as all that, and I haven't even met
Signor Vittorini.'

'When you do, you'll fall for him,' Stacey declared
confidently.

'I'm afraid that's extremely unlikely.'

Stacey sighed. 'Wish I was old enough to marry him,'
she murmured.

'Pity you aren't,' Francesca agreed, stirring her coffee.

'How old do you have to be to get married?' Stacey
asked.

'In England sixteen. I don't know about out here,
but you've a long way to go, honey, and by the time
you get there he'll be getting on, and you'll have
changed your mind.'

'I don't think so,' Stacey insisted. 'But it would be
nearly as good if he married you, for then he'd be my
brother.'

Francesca made no comment on that; she was wondering how old Angelo Vittorini actually was. It was

unusual, if he were any age at all, that he should be still unattached. Heir to an important property and his father's business interests, it would be expected of him to perpetuate his line at an early date, especially as he had no brothers. So far he seemed to have been able to evade his responsibilities, but now he had been persuaded to assume them, doubtless intending to return to his former amusements as soon as possible. He had evidently put in some spadework with her family before her coming, ingratiating himself with her parents and capturing her sister's fancy. Yet it was surprising that he considered Bellavista worth the effort, but his father was sentimental about it. The Marchese set so much store upon the place that he was ready to accept an unknown foreign girl as his son's wife.

He did not know that the property would soon be on the market, and his ignorance of the true circumstances was Henry's trump card. Actually her father was being dishonest, but she could not bring herself to blame him, for he was in a desperate situation and he must find her obduracy exasperating. He stood to gain so much if only she would fall in with his plans. She stared up at the palms motionless in the still air. Desmond had failed her and the Vittorinis were making a very generous offer, so much so that if she accepted she would feel beholden to them for the rest of her life. An intolerable position, she thought resentfully.

Then she remembered that her grandmother had also sponsored the match, and she had been the Marchese's friend. In her own veins ran an eighth of the Italian blood inherited from her great-grandmother, with whom the Vittorinis shared a common ancestor, but why had she never mentioned it to her, had in fact avoided a meeting between the two young people?

Thinking about it, Francesca realised that this evasiveness was typical of her grandmother. She had the Latin love of intrigue and approached her objectives under cover. Too early a meeting might have prejudiced her schemes, especially if the young man's interest had been engaged elsewhere. As his father had done, she had waited for him to be finished with sowing his wild oats, and a hint of her intentions might have put Francesca against him. She had relied upon an introduction under auspicious circumstances, and the charm of an experienced man of the world to overcome any reluctance upon the girl's part. Francesca smiled wryly. Desmond's appearance had threatened to put a spoke in the wheel of all this careful planning, but although annoyed, the elder Francesca had confined her opposition to an insistence that the girl was too young to think of marriage. Had she suspected that Francesca's feeling for Desmond was not deep and that sooner or later she would see through his shallow pretensions?

So she had bided her time, seemingly acquiescent, and refrained from all mention of Angelo Vittorini, until the Desmond interlude should evaporate and her granddaughter be ready to be caught on the rebound. Devious, far-sighted old lady, at least with regard to Desmond she had been proved right.

Francesca sighed. Like all young girls she had dreamed of romantic love, though her grandmother had insisted that it was a chimera. As she grew older she had come to doubt its existence in a prosaic world. Certainly the way love was cheapened among her acquaintances reduced it to a mere appetite, to be appeased like hunger, thirst and all the other bodily needs, and that was how Desmond regarded it. But in spite of the cynicism and self-gratification she saw on every side, she could not accept it as such. Her father she knew had always adored her mother, despite the irritation of her constant ailments. But she distrusted violent emotions; she had thought the affection she felt towards Desmond was more likely to prove durable than an infatuation.

Her father came on to the terrace, his face drawn with worry. Stella, he said, had had a bad night. While they had been in Italy, she had had no recurrence of her illness, but now she was threatened with an acute attack. Asthma was a curious complaint; it could be brought on by emotional conflict and mental disturbance. He looked reproachfully at Francesca.

She felt a stab of compunction. She had only to say one word and the worry would lift from her father's face, her mother would recover and Stacey would be happy. It was the child's position which bore most weight with her. She could do so much for her if she agreed, and now there was no Desmond to present a barrier.

He brightened when Stacey told him that the young man had gone and looked questioningly at his daughter.

'He remembered something he'd forgotten in Imperia,' Francesca said, purposely vague.

'He'll be coming back?'

'I don't think so, it's a long way up here.' Anxious not to nurture false hopes, she added: 'We'll be meeting again in London soon.'

His face clouded, and Stacey announced vehemently:

'I didn't like that man.'

'You don't know him,' Francesca rebuked her. 'And he's my friend, not yours.'

But he was no longer that. True friends did not run away from trouble. Would Desmond offer any explanation beyond that cryptic note? Could he offer any explanation for his desertion?

A diversion was caused by the arrival of a servant from the Castello bringing a note from his master inviting the family to lunch.

'Me too?' Stacey asked anxiously as Henry read the missive which was addressed to him and his wife.

'Yes, little one, he includes you.' He looked at Francesca doubtfully. 'You won't refuse to come?'

'I'll be pleased to,' she told him. She knew it would be considered very rude if she did not go. The writing paper was thick and expensive, the envelope sealed with a crest. Since their telephone had been cut off pending payment of the account, the Marchese had no option but to write.

Stella made an immediate recovery upon receiving this invitation, and penned a reply for the waiting servant. She then proceeded to review her shabby wardrobe with may sighs.

'At least there is no Marchesa to criticise my clothes,' she said thankfully. 'The Marchese has been a widower for many years.'

'So I've been told,' Francesca told her tartly. 'I'm only surprised he didn't propose himself as my husband, since it's the land he's after.'

Stella gave her daughter an oblique glance. Standing in the full sunshine, slender as a willow wand in her slacks and sleeveless shirt, her hair tumbling about her shoulders, Francesca was a radiant vision of youth.

'Perhaps he will,' she murmured, 'if Angelo doesn't come up to scratch.'

Francesca was startled. 'I thought it was all signed and sealed pending my consent.'

With unusual perspicacity, Stella remarked:

'With hot-blooded youngsters, nothing is ever certain.'

This observation Francesca took in the nature of a challenge. That Angelo might be as reluctant as she was herself to fall in with his father's wishes was a new idea and with feminine perversity, she became determined to impress him. She chose a silk dress, one of the many her grandmother had given her, a midi-skirted affair in pale green falling in soft folds from a high waist, with long chiffon sleeves. With it she wore a large picture hat and white gloves, knowing Italians were formal on social occasions.

Stacey thoroughly disapproved of her appearance.

'You look so old-fashioned,' she exclaimed. 'I thought you'd wear something more with-it.'

'I've an idea the Marchese will appreciate the old-world touch,' Francesca said drily. 'I don't suppose minis and trousers are his idea of feminine wear, and so the lamb is suitably decked for the slaughter.'

This remark being beyond her, Stacey turned her attention to her own clothes.

'Do I look nice? This frock's awfully old.'

It was white, so at least it did not look faded as most of the child's dresses did, and the hem had obviously been let down, but the anxious little face above it was sweet and winsome, and her hair, for once well brushed, a golden aureole.

'It's clean and fresh, and you look charming,' Francesca told her. If she married Angelo the child could have a whole new wardrobe.

The Castello on its spur of rock looked formidable as they drove the Fiat up to its massive honey-coloured walls, the main entrance being on the seaward side. A wide gateway led into a courtyard filled with potted plants, around which the building was disposed in a square. Standing above the hills between it and the sea, the Mediterranean could be glimpsed from its walls, upon which its defenders had watched for the approach of marauders. On the inland side, overlooking Bellavista, the escarpment was terraced with lengths of green lawns, ornamental trees and several statues. The main rooms were upon this side, modern windows having replaced the old narrow ones, with a paved terrace beneath them, and a fine view across the shallow valley to the mountains.

As they got out of the Fiat in the courtyard, the Marchese came to greet them, shaking hands solemnly with each in turn. He led them into a vast hall with a marble floor, and across it on to the terrace. Here an awning had been spread and it was furnished with coloured cane chairs and a canopied swinging lounger, upon which Stacey promptly ensconced herself.

'My son will be here shortly,' Antonio Vittorini told them. He spoke English with only a trace of accent. His keen eyes under their beetling brows were openly appraising Francesca, but he addressed his conversation to her mother. The Temples were a little over-awed by the sombre magnificence of their surroundings; even Stacey was subdued. She whispered to her sister who had sat down beside her:

'I usually go to the kitchen—it's nicer there.'

I'm sure it is, Francesca thought, it would be less formal. The Marchese appeared to live in a former age and the Castello struck cold and unfriendly upon the impressionable girl. She could not imagine living a normal life in this stately setting, served by soft-footed servants of which there seemed to be no lack. The whole atmosphere of the place was unreal. The Dukes of Milan might have felt at home there, but not a twentieth-century girl.

Signor Vittorini kept throwing impatient glances towards the door into the house.

'I do not know why Angelo delays,' he muttered. 'The *pranzo* will spoil.'

He summoned his butler—major-domo or whatever the fellow was—by ringing a bell and enquired in Italian for his son. The impressive-looking personage shrugged and rolled his eyes. The movements of Signor Angelo were unpredictable. Their host became full of apologies, some unforeseen occurrence no doubt had delayed him, but the deep set eyes were sparkling angrily. They would wait no longer. He offered his arm to Stella, who took it with a simper. The others followed. Francesca suspected Angelo was no more anxious to make her acquaintance than she was his—correction, she did want to see what he was like, but his dilatoriness was unflattering.

The dining room was a large high-ceilinged room furnished with a polished table and carved chairs. There were portraits on the walls of former Vittorinis, a huge carved fireplace occupied one wall; sunblinds shielded the enlarged windows from the heat of the sun, and vases of roses stood on the table. On the carved sideboard were two big vases of Faenza ware, glowing with colour. Francesca found it oppressive; she could not visualise coming down to breakfast in that huge room. Was there nowhere in the castle where one could relax, or did the Vittorinis never relax? She had an uneasy suspicion that they did not. Their existence was a dignified façade erected against the sharp eyes of their own servants.

The Marchese sat at the head of his table with Stella on his right and Francesca on his left. Her father was placed beside her, and beyond him Stacey. There was an empty place next to her mother opposite to her.

The butler carved and superintended the efforts of an elderly maidservant who waited upon them. The Marchese and Henry discussed olive harvesting in great detail, while the women listened meekly.

The food was good and well prepared—*minestrone alla Genovise*, a soup seasoned with *pisto*, followed by *fritto allo stecco*, a dish comprised of veal, sweetbreads, brains and mushrooms dipped in egg yolks and crumbs, and then fried. Their host informed them that in addition to his chef, he employed an excellent housekeeper, who had been with the family for years, and the household ran on oiled wheels. What on earth would one do all day, Francesca wondered, since every chore was performed for one? She could not see herself existing in such surroundings, for presumably Angelo would continue to live with his father. She would die of ennui or stifled by empty pomp. She threw an agonised glance at her father, who was savouring his *fritto* and his Chianti. How could he bear to condemn her to such a fate? Then she realised that he was enjoying the best meal he had eaten for many a long day and was struck with mingled pity and exasperation. At his age and that of the Marchese, material comforts became all-important, but she was young, and food and wine were no compensation for lack of liberty.

'*Scusi, scusi, mio padre, sono molto dispiacente*—I was delayed— *Comé sta, signore, signori?* How are you, little one?' This to Stacey.

They had not heard him come in, but suddenly he was there, bowing and offering his greetings and excuses in Italian and English. With his coming the whole atmosphere seemed to change, to become alive. The Marchese looked up frowning, but his frown was dissipated in a fond smile, as he looked proudly at this son of his; the Temples visibly brightened, while

79

Stacey gave an ecstatic squeal of 'Angelo!'

As for Francesca, that arrow-straight figure, broad of shoulder, slender of hip, wearing in defiance of convention a thin black sweater and narrow black trousers, was not unfamiliar, neither was the firm chin and aquiline nose, but the eyes, which for the first time she beheld unmasked, were deep velvet pools, so dark that the pupils were indistinguishable from the iris, set under slanting black brows and surrounded by lashes as long as spiders' legs, giving a deceptive suggestion of softness to his regular features, which had the hard perfection of a classical statue. While he apologised, in that deep pleasant voice, which was also familiar, his eyes swept over Francesca with a sleepy sensuous look which made her heart flutter; even while it did so, she suspected that it was a practised look, and he knew the effect it had upon feminine susceptibilities.

So this was Angelo Vittorini, who designed his own sports car, and who had come to the Calvis' dance disguised as the Devil—a suitable dress, for his was the beauty of a fallen angel; even in his everyday garb there was something vaguely Satanic about him. His appearance apparently did not meet with his father's approval, for he made some objection in his own tongue.

'I did not wait to change,' Angelo explained, with a flashing smile which showed his fine white teeth, 'that would have made me even later. Please to excuse my unconventional get-up.' He bowed to Stella. 'We are after all old friends and we can therefore dispense with formalities.'

The Marchese frowned, for correct dress was considered part of good manners. He began coldly: 'You have not met the Signorina Temple. May I present ...'

'Oh, but I have,' Angelo almost purred. 'Twice.' He

smiled at Francesca with devastating charm. 'I am delighted to welcome you to my ancestral home.' He bowed again with foreign grace, and took his place beside Stella.

The others looked surprised, and Francesca said a little scornfully:

'It's the first time we've met under your true colours, Signor Vittorini. Hitherto I hadn't the pleasure of knowing either your identity or your status.'

'At a masked ball one does not disclose either, or what would be the point in wearing a mask?' Angelo pointed out.

'But you were conspicuously absent when we unmasked. Giulia Calvi thought you were a gatecrasher.'

He laughed. 'So much more romantic that you shouldn't discover my name until now,' he said suavely.

'I don't see what was the point of concealing it.'

'Do you not? Perhaps you dream a little about the red devil, and wonder, but if you knew I was only your neighbour . . .' He shrugged expressively.

'Red devil?' Stacey demanded, round-eyed. 'Did you go as a devil, Angelo?'

'As Mephistopheles.'

'So appropriate,' Francesca murmured, her eyes challenging his.

'Perhaps, but I told you we would meet again, and you see we have.'

He turned his attention to the food being offered to him, while Francesca sought to collect her whirling thoughts. To discover that Angelo had been the mocking devil of the incident at the ball had come as a shock. She had very nearly decided that if Angelo Vittorini were at all presentable, she would fall in with her father's wishes, but then he had been an abstraction. At best she had expected a younger edition of his father, a courteous, polished participant in a marriage of convenience, but Angelo had now become a living personality and a very disturbing one. Nor could she credit that he would meekly fall in with his father's plans unless he was strongly inclined to do so, and she could see no reason why he should be.

Coffee and liqueurs were served on the terrace, and as they left the dining room, the Marchese spoke urgently aside to his son. Angelo shrugged his shoulders.

'*Va bene*,' he waved a careless hand in the Temples' direction. 'I will join you in a few moments.'

Stacey whispered to her sister, 'Isn't he nice?'

'If you mean Signor Angelo, that's hardly the word I should use,' Francesca told her, with a bright spot of colour in either cheek.

Stacey looked dashed. 'Didn't you like him?'

'That again isn't quite the right word.' Like and nice were anaemic descriptions of the vivid personality that had just left them. Other words presented themselves to Francesca's mind—arresting, magnetic, disconcerting, even theatrical, but she could not explain them to the child.

Angelo came back. Evidently he had been commanded to make himself more presentable. The perfectly fitting grey suit he had put on changed him from a daredevil to a man about town. Shirt, tie, shoes were well chosen and immaculate, the only foreign touch the black broad-brimmed hat he carried. His father nodded approval.

'I was, you see, investigating the intestines of my car,' Angelo explained. 'I could hardly wear my best suit to do that.'

'Why embark upon such a messy job when visitors were expected?' the Marchese asked.

Angelo looked contrite. 'I am afraid I had forgotten.'

Francesca reflected that he had found his machine much more interesting than the arrival of his prospective bride.

Refusing coffee, he bowed to Francesca and asked: 'Would the *signorina* care to inspect the gardens?'

Francesca rose reluctantly, picking up her hat which lay on the seat beside her, for the sun was strong. No use procrastinating; she might as well hear what he had to say, and get it over. Stacey hinted that she would like to accompany them, but was bidden to stay where she was. Angelo put his hat on his head at a rakish angle and offered Francesca his arm with a mocking smile to guide her down the steps leading to the garden.

'Thank you, but I can manage,' she said coolly.

He raised his eyebrows, but did not insist. They moved sedately down a flight of marble stairs, the girl a slender nymph in pale green, the man a grey shadow beside her.

They crossed a lawn, the green of which was preserved by sprinklers, the only green in a landscape of browns and mauves. Angelo glanced back at the Castello behind them and the group upon the terrace.

'What do you think of the mausoleum?' he asked.

'It's a bit ... overwhelming.'

He laughed. 'A relic of a bygone era, but my father loves it. He likes to live in old-fashioned state, a remnant of a feudal age, but I should prefer a villa on the coast.' He glanced at her obliquely. 'And probably you would too.'

Francesca turned her head away, glad that her big hat shaded it. So he was prepared to agree to this cold-hearted bargain, but her whole being rose up in rebellion against the fate proposed for her. It was alien to her experience, and not the least alien element was the man beside her.

They walked along a broad gravelled path lined with statuary. At the end of it a shrubbery of mimosa trees, feathery of foliage, their blossoming over, concealed a secluded spot with marble benches surrounding a mass of flowering rose bushes, among which a stone Cupid was poised, his arrow drawn to his bow. Angelo indicated it.

'Eros,' he said with a mischievous grin. 'And all ready to shoot.' He peeled off his elegant jacket and spread it over the marble seat. 'Sit down, *cara mia*, that will protect you from the heat of the bench, which has been broiling in the sun, and let us proceed to business.'

The sunshine and heavy scent from the roses wrapped them round in sensuous languor. She seated herself demurely where he indicated, wondering what she was going to say to him.

Angelo glanced at her uncertainly, then with a dramatic gesture, which concealed a slight embarrassment, went down on one knee before her.

'Most exquisite, fair and unmatchable beauty,' he declaimed, while his black eyes danced with mischief: 'You see I can quote your English bard. Behold me at your feet. I, Angelo Giovanni Sebastiano Vittorini, having attained nearly thirty years, future owner of the Castello and all its acres, a director of the oil company—oh yes, I have been promoted to that honour—a man neither better nor worse than other men, but commanded by fate in the person of my august father to take you to wife. All that is mine shall be yours, including—ahem—my heart. I suppose you are agreeable?'

84

His eyes glinted up at her, but in spite of his humble attitude there was no humility in him. Her answer was a foregone conclusion.

'Get up, you look ridiculous,' she said sharply. 'There's no need for the play-acting.' He rose, dusting his knees. 'I don't think I am agreeable,' she went on. 'The whole proceeding is so cold-blooded.'

Sheer astonishment showed in his eyes, but only for a moment; instantly he quenched it. Evidently her hesitation was unexpected.

'I daresay that can be amended,' he suggested. 'But the midday sunshine is a little too revealing. We need moonlight and shadows like the last time we were together—besides, I find difficulty in making love in my best clothes.' He glanced ruefully at the crease in his trousers.

'You prefer the devil's get-up?' she returned, aware of an inner excitement for which she despised herself. Sexually he was alluring and he knew it. He would use all his armoury to get his own way, or more correctly his father's way.

He was studying her through half closed eyes, assessing her point by point, and she flushed uncomfortably.

'I think it became me,' he said complacently. 'As yours did you, my little moon maiden, but today you are more like a flower with a long green stalk, *molta bella.*'

Ignoring this flight of fancy, she said accusingly:

'You knew then who I was and what was intended?'

'But of course, and do you blame me if I wanted to inspect the merchandise before I bid for it?'

'And you decided it was worth having?' Outwardly very demure, the curve of her lips was provocative.

His eyes smouldered. 'Definitely.'

'Well, that's nice to know. Let's quit the trimmings, and suppose you sit down.' His dark presence looming over her was disconcerting.

He obeyed, taking his place beside her and she wished she had not suggested it, finding his close proximity was causing her nerves to quiver. Making an effort to speak calmly, she went on:

'You've made a very generous offer and for my family's sake I should perhaps accept it, but I can't see what you're getting out of it. Your father wants Bellavista, but I should not think that was of much interest to you. I'm a very ordinary girl and a foreigner at that. Nor do I love you, my heart is involved elsewhere.' His mouth twisted in an ironical smile; he did not believe there was much truth in that statement. 'I'm a precious poor bargain from your point of view,' she finished deprecatingly.

'You are too modest,' he returned. 'I find you quite enchanting, and since I have to have a wife, I consider myself fortunate. I might have had to wed some homely Italian girl, who would become fat.' He hesitated, then spoke more seriously, his eyes searching her face. 'This man with whom your heart is involved ... he makes love to you?'

Francesca turned her head away, aware that she had flushed. 'Not seriously.'

He put his hand under her chin and brought her round to face him; her clear candid eyes met his probing glance wonderingly.

'That is evident, you are still asleep,' he told her, and as the wild rose colour rose again in her face, he added: 'Not the least of your considerable attractions is your obvious innocence.'

He must think she was very unsophisticated, she thought with annoyance, and said provocatively: 'The jealous Italian again?'

'The Vittorinis are jealous of their women's honour,' he said proudly, and murmured *sotto voce*, 'A man likes to be sure his children are his own.'

He had not intended her to overhear his last sentence, but her quick ears caught it, and her face flamed at the implication.

'Signor Vittorini,' she began.

'Angelo,' he interrupted.

'Signor Vittorini,' she repeated firmly. 'You're galloping ahead. I don't think I can bring myself to accept this . . . this bargain.'

The black eyes staring into hers flickered and became black stones.

'You play with me? Surely no girl in her right senses would hesitate to accept such advantages? Is it that you are trying to provoke me to greater ardour?'

She pushed his hand away, incensed that he was taking her consent for granted.

'I don't want your ardour,' she said coldly, and again his eyelids flickered. 'You're a stranger, we don't love each other, and yet you expect me to accept a bond which in your country lasts for a lifetime.'

'Ah, love!' He glanced quizzically at the statue of Eros with his drawn bow. 'You wish to wait until Cupid has struck you with his dart? Like all young *signorinas* you dream of romance? Believe me, romance is much over-rated, material comforts are far more satisfactory. Besides, you have already been transfixed by one of his arrows, have you not?' She turned her head away to conceal the trembling of her lips. Desmond's sudden flight had wounded her, his love had failed her.

Angelo said softly, 'He has deserted you, has he not?'

'He had to go away suddenly,' she murmured, anxious to conceal from him her hurt. 'He may return.'

'He will not. The fear of being saddled with your impecunious family has scared him off, besides...' He checked himself. No need for her to know that he had warned the young man not to show his face at Bellavista again.

She winced at his words, which she feared were true, but he could not know that; she believed he was only guessing, and had no sure knowledge to support his assertion. She turned round to face him squarely, and noticed with a qualm the ruthless set of his mouth. He would not be easy to thwart once his purpose was set.

'Please leave him out of it,' she bade him. 'Apparently you are ready to provide for my family and I should be grateful to you for that, but it is entirely for their sake that I'm prepared to consider this ... this alliance, and if, knowing that, you still want to go through with it, and you realise that I don't and never will love you as a wife should love...' She broke off, twisting her hands together.

'Never is a very final word,' he said gravely. 'In my class and country we do not look for love before marriage, but it frequently develops afterwards.'

So he anticipated that she would be unable to resist his charms, that she would succumb in the end.

'Don't kid yourself it will between us,' she warned him tensely. 'I ... I would do my duty, of course.' She turned pale as she thought what those duties would entail. 'But I would never be able to forget that I was bought.'

'In many parts of the world men still buy their wives with cattle and camels,' he returned flippantly. 'How many head of cattle do you consider you are worth?' Laughter was in his eyes again.

'Quite a herd, I should imagine.'

'Oh, you can laugh!' she exclaimed, indignant because he did not take her assertions seriously.

'It is better than crying, which is what you seem about to do. It is no compliment to a man when a woman weeps at the prospect of receiving his embraces.'

There was an almost savage undercurrent to his words and Francesca shivered. 'I am afraid that is the nature of a man, and I am no exception,' he went on harshly. 'That is the price you must pay for the salvation of your precious family, and it seems you find it too high.'

She bowed her head, biting her lips. He was perceptive enough to have noticed her aversion, and had been stung by it.

'I hardly know you,' she whispered, 'and I'm not susceptible to Latin charm.'

Bending his head to catch her words, he said softly, 'So you consider I have charm? That is flattering, *cara mia*, and you may be sure that if you recognised it now, you will eventually succumb to it.'

'You are too confident.' She drew away from him. 'But there's no need to go on with this. I must be honest with you.' She drew a deep breath, for she hated having to expose her father, but she felt Angelo was being cheated. 'I'm ashamed to have to tell you this. My father is bluffing you. Bellavista is heavily mortgaged and he can't pay the interest. The property will have to be sold, and your father can pick it up for a song, so there's no need for you to involve yourself with me.'

Angelo gave her a long enigmatical look.

'So you think that it is only to gain Bellavista that I wish to marry you?'

'Isn't it? I can't think of any other reason.'

89

'Can you not?' His eyes lingered on the silky flow of her hair, under her big hat, her chiselled features, and came to rest on the curves of her mouth, a mouth which held infinite promise of rapture, when its owner had learned to give herself wholeheartedly. 'Do you not know that your grandmother planned our marriage with my father when we were still children?'

'So I've been told, but only recently, but there again, the idea was to join the properties, wasn't it? When it was mooted, Bellavista was prosperous.'

'You seem obsessed by Bellavista,' he observed.

'It's the crux of the matter, isn't it?'

'Not at all. My father had a high opinion of your grandmother, and he knew you would be well brought up.' He glanced at her obliquely. 'I came home to take up the option, so to speak, but insisted that I must see you first.'

'Very wise of you,' she agreed demurely. 'When you picked me up when the Fiat broke down, you knew who I was?'

'I did. Let me tell you I don't pick up, as you say, all and sundry. It's too equivocal.'

She remembered the intimacy of the confined space of the sports car and blushed faintly.

'Your first sight of me couldn't have been very prepossessing,' she suggested, for she had been dusty and untidy and he had seen her, as it were, through a glass darkly.

'I saw what I wanted to see,' he returned enigmatically.

He leaned against the back of the seat, and asked:

'What do you propose to do if you do not marry me?'

'We'll all have to go back to England,' she told him. 'I don't quite know what our circumstances will be, but I can earn good money as a cook.'

He gave a startled exclamation, and she went on serenely:

'I've reached Cordon Bleu standard and I daresay I can do a lot towards helping them.'

He picked up her hand, looking at the slim, white fingers and filbert nails, and a tremor went through her at his action.

'Desecration!' he ejaculated.

She snatched her hand away from him.

'My grandmother may have brought me up soft, but that doesn't mean I can't cope with earning a living.'

'Independent,' he murmured, 'and courageous. But it is a dreary prospect, *cara mia*. I do not like to think of you struggling to support your poverty-stricken family.'

'I feel responsible for them.'

He leaned towards her. 'Am I so repulsive to you that you would rather work those delicate fingers to the bone than let me take care of you all?'

'No, I didn't mean that, but . . . why should you?'

An impish light danced in his eyes. 'Let us say I have a whim to play the public benefactor and I have a fancy for pale gold hair.'

'Oh, really, *signore*!' She did not know whether to laugh or cry. 'Those don't seem very adequate reasons for marriage.'

'No?' He drew back, looking away from her into the sunlit distance. 'I am very fond of Anastasia, I would like to give the child the advantages she deserves.'

'Ah, Stacey!' she breathed, her face softening.

'She loves Italy, and it will be painful for her to leave, your mother too is delicate, the British climate might kill her.'

Francesca moved restlessly. 'I know all that. It's a

form of blackmail my father has already applied.'

He looked at her out of eyes that had become soft as black velvet, and were full of reproach.

'You use harsh words, *cara*, and I am grieved that your aversion to myself causes you to use them. Can it be that you are still seeing me as the red devil at the masked ball?'

Again she turned in her seat to face him squarely. His olive face was inscrutable, but now in the depths of his eyes a tiny flame seemed to burn.

'You're ready to do an awful lot for me,' she said wonderingly. 'But I'm not worth it, you know.'

'That is for me to judge.' The black lashes veiled his eyes. 'If I were more explicit, I might shock your innocence.'

A shiver ran up her spine. 'I'm not completely unsophisticated. I know men can feel desire without love.'

He stiffened at this observation, which seemed to offend him. Ignoring it, he said coldly:

'May I have your answer to my proposal, Signorina Temple? Or do you need time to consider it? My father is expecting us to return to him engaged.'

Francesca checked the negative upon her lips, for her first impulse was to refuse him. Her future prospects were not alluring. She would have a hard struggle to cope with her family, and his offer to take the burden from her shoulders if accepted would mean an enormous relief. She was still sore from Desmond's desertion, and it was a sop to know that this man, whatever his reasons wanted her; an attractive man, whose admiration was flattering to her wounded ego, and to whom, if she were honest, Desmond could only be compared unfavourably in looks and bearing. She might accede to the point of becoming engaged. Engagements were a trial period, and not irrevocable. She might in time be able to reconcile herself to this marriage, and if she could not, the betrothal could be broken off.

'Very well, *signore*,' she told him. 'I ... I accept your generosity,' and was disconcerted by the unmistakable flash of triumph in his eyes. 'But ... but if I find I can't go through with it...' There was a desperate appeal in her violet eyes.

He asked: 'You will want me to release you?'

'Yes. Will you promise to do so?'

He hesitated, then said: 'Yes, if that is your condition, but I shall endeavour to persuade you to go through with it.'

Having gained her point, she said demurely: 'Thank you, *signore*.'

'Had not you better call me Angelo?' he suggested. 'An inappropriate name, I know, but there are dark angels as well as shining ones.'

She smiled wanly. 'Lucifer?' she murmured.

'Or Mephistopheles. And that reminds me, you still owe me a debt, Francesca.'

Her eyes widened in alarm. 'I ... I suppose you consider you have the right...'

'Ah no, I wouldn't enforce it as a right.' The so dark eyes were pleading. 'Could you not think of me a little more kindly, Francesca?'

His reproach moved her. For reasons which she could not wholly understand, he was proposing to do an enormous amount for her, and yet she baulked at a kiss.

'Oh, I will,' she cried, and impulsively put her arms about his neck. His caress, a mere pressure of her lips, was very gentle, and almost at once he disengaged himself.

'You are like strong wine,' he said huskily, and sprang to his feet, holding out his hand to her. 'Come, *amore mia*, let us give them the good news.'

She laid hers in his, feeling the action was symbolical.

'You said our lives were linked,' she reminded him. 'Then I didn't understand, but now I do.'

'May the link never be broken,' he said fervently. He scooped up his jacket from the seat with his free hand, and still holding hers, led her back towards the Castello.

CHAPTER FIVE

HAVING become engaged to Angelo Vittorini with the idea that if she found him insupportable she could break it off, Francesca soon discovered that she had enmeshed herself in a web from which it would be almost impossible to extricate herself. She had reckoned without the Marchese's patriarchal instincts.

A descendant of the old nobility, bearing an ancient name, he had in his youth, in common with many of his age and class, renounced his title, declaring himself a member of the bourgeoisie, and devoted his energies to the olive oil business. But in his middle years tradition caught up with him. His parents died, the Castello descended squarely upon his shoulders with all the demands of his peasantry, who looked up to him with feudal loyalty. After his wife's death, he went less and less to the factory, immersing himself in the country pursuits followed by his ancestors and trying to improve the lot of his villagers in an attempt to check the drift to the towns. His brother had died unwed in an accident, his only child was Angelo, who, as soon as he attained maturity, was rarely at home. Antonio Vittorini hungered for a crowd of descendants looking up to him for direction. The heart of Italian life was the family, and that included all its branches. Far from regarding the Temples as an imposition, he considered it was only natural to provide for them since they were to be his connections, and he revived the claim of a common ancestor, whose existence had never been fully ratified, to prove that they were kin.

He busied himself manoeuvring their lives. Bellavista, he declared, was an unsuitable residence for Stella; she should be lodged in a flat near the coast—a suggestion that she accepted with delight. The hilly road up to Castel Vecchio made walking impossible for her and she could not drive the Fiat. She was hungry for shops and people. Henry was offered a position with the firm in the correspondence department where his knowledge of both Italian and English would be an asset. This he accepted with alacrity. Stacey was to go to a convent school, a prospect against which she rebelled violently. Angelo was deputed to persuade her to go, which he did successfully, telling her that he wanted her to become a cultivated woman whom he would be proud to call his sister. She would have holidays, he pointed out, which she could, if she wished, spend at the Castello, and Bruno could be housed there and well tended.

Regarding Angelo himself, he appeared to be in the process of settling down, as his father had requested. His precious sports model seemed to have disappeared. When he drove Francesca anywhere, he used his father's Ferrari. The casinos of San Remo and Monte Carlo knew him no more, and when he was not in the oil company's offices he was at Castel Vecchio superintending the cultivations.

With all these plans depending upon her marriage, and Angelo's reformation, Francesca felt she was well and truly caught, and it would be well nigh impossible to draw back. Sensibly she decided to make the best of the situation which was so satisfactory to everybody else, and to endeavour to get to know her future husband, which was far from easy. Although he was a considerate and attentive fiancé, he held himself aloof, and she could find no key to his complex personality. Contrary to her expectations, he made no physical demands upon her, confining his demonstrations to kissing her fingertips, a formal salutation, so that she might almost have supposed that he was indifferent to her—almost but not quite. For often he watched her with that slumbrous, sensuous expression in his eyes, which made her heart quicken its beat, and made her think of a predatory animal watching its intended prey. She suspected that he was only waiting for the time when she was officially his to give rein to the full force of his desire. She awaited the approach of that day with mingled apprehension and excitement, and it would come soon, for there was no reason for delay.

Neither of them wished for a big wedding. Only the Temples and a few old friends of the Vittorinis had been asked to attend the ceremony in the old church next door to the Castello.

Angelo was determined that they would not live there, though his father had wanted them to do so. He proposed to rent a villa near the coast, and to his father's protests, he had simply said:

'I wish to be with my bride alone, *padre mio.*'

That the elder man could understand.

'But you will come back eventually to the home of your ancestors?' he insisted. 'The *bambini* should be raised where they belong.'

Angelo had merely smiled.

To Francesca he admitted that he found the Castello far too old-fashioned and oppressive, and much too large. At his father's death he proposed to make it into a show-piece for visitors, or a hotel.

'But we, *cara,* require something more modern and accessible.'

With which she heartily concurred.

He took her to inspect various white-walled, red-roofed houses in the newest designs, and the one which pleased her most was on the hill overlooking Diano Marina, the next township eastward along the coast. Set among palm trees and umbrella pines, with a shaded patio roofed with vine, a flight of steps led up to the front door, above a garage and the kitchens. The big window of the *salotto* looked out across the bay over the town to the next headland. A balcony ran along the front of the house on to which it opened. Behind it rose the hillside dotted with trees, including the ubiquitous olive.

'You like it? You could be happy here?' Angelo asked.

'I'm sure I could. It's lovely.' She looked at him gratefully. 'You're very good to me, Angelo.'

He smiled a little wryly. 'You will reward me no doubt when the time comes,' he suggested meaningly.

She flushed painfully and turned her head away.

'I'll do my best.' But there was no warmth in her voice, and she pleated her dress between nervous fingers. Angelo studied her with a slight frown. They were standing on the balcony outside the *salotto*. The sun poured down upon the girl, illuminating her fair hair, so that it shone like silver gilt; her white dress and pure profile gave her a virginal appearance. He wondered if she were frigid, but the curves of her mouth belied such a supposition. In spite of the episode with Desmond, he guessed she was still unawakened. It would be his privilege to arouse her, and his breathing quickened at the prospect. Francesca glanced at him in time to catch his expression, and a trapped look crept into her beautiful eyes.

'*Dio mio!*' Angelo exclaimed violently. 'Are you afraid of me, Francesca?'

She laughed nervously. 'Not really, only ... well, I've never been married before.'

'But you would not have been apprehensive with that other fellow?' he asked, and she sensed his jealousy.

'I knew him so much better than I do you,' she pointed out.

He threw out his hands in exasperation.

'What can I do to make you know me better? To kill this fear in you, for you are frightened, *cara mia*, and yet I am not a bogey.'

'Of course not.' But he was an alien, of a different race and tradition, and there was some element in him which repelled her, even while it fascinated her. He was the descendant of an ancient family that had stained the pages of its history with bloodshed and treachery, and she sensed a hidden violence beneath his surface urbanity, that had never been wholly tamed.

'You ... you're so different from ... me,' she said uncertainly. She had nearly said Desmond, but checked herself in time. References to the other man were better avoided. Nor could she explain the inexplicable. She looked around at the charming house, the beautiful view. Even now it did not seem possible that she was really going to live here alone with him.

'In time I shall become familiar,' he told her drily. 'And familiarity, they say, breeds contempt.'

'That I'm sure I could never feel for you,' she declared.

'Which is at least satisfactory,' he was still dry. 'A wife should venerate her husband.'

'They don't ... always.' She smiled provocatively. 'Not when they get to know them too well. Angelo, have there been ... many other women?'

'None that counted. Does that worry you?' He looked almost eager.

99

'Not particularly.' A shade of—was it disappointment? crossed his face. He had hoped she would show jealousy of his former loves. 'I've heard gossip,' she went on casually. 'I just wondered.'

'I see. Unfortunately I managed to attract a certain amount of limelight, and what in other men's lives would have been mere episodes were magnified into lurid affairs.' He paused. 'There will be no more after we are married,' he told her firmly.

'Italians are not famed for constancy.'

'That is mere hearsay. You must not condemn me because of some absurd national prejudice. No doubt you have been told that I am wild and irresponsible. Most young men are if they have the opportunity. But my roving days are done, I intend to become a model citizen, so you need have no qualms, if that is what troubles you.'

It was not. She had given scant consideration to Angelo's past since she had become engaged to him. It was the future, the close intimacy which she must share with him, which was much more disturbing.

'I only hope you won't come to regret marrying me,' she said faintly.

'I am sure I will never do that,' he told her fervently.

Having decided that they would take the villa, Angelo drove her back to Bellavista, where they gave her parents a rapturous description of their new home.

Francesca felt as if she were living in a dream; nothing was quite real. The half hoop of diamonds that she wore, which Angelo had given her, was a beautiful and expensive ring. Everything belonging to him seemed to be expensive and beautiful. He told her that he took a connoisseur's pleasure in such things and was grateful for the wealth which enabled him to surround himself with them. She thought wryly that she was the latest addition to his collection, for though not vain, she would have been a fool not to know that men found her fair, especially dark ones, to whom her fragile blondeness had an irresistible appeal. Had she been plain, there would have been no proposal, Bellavista notwithstanding. She demurred when he bought her jewels, and was embarrassed by the interest he took in what she wore. She was not yet his wife, and the costly gifts he showered upon her made her feel like a harem slave, bedecked to please his critical eye. He knew far too much about feminine gear, and she suspected the ladies belonging to those 'episodes' had educated him in that respect. On the other hand it was flattering that he noticed everything she put on and complimented her when she met with his approval, Desmond had always been indifferent to her appearance so long as she looked what he called nice.

The person who was most elated by the turn of events was her sister. Even the dreaded prospect of school could not quench her triumph.

'I knew you'd fall for Angelo,' she reiterated, 'and you did, almost at once. Aren't you lucky, Fran, that he fell in love with you?'

She had forgotten that pressure had been put upon Francesca, and saw their engagement as a glorious technicolor romance. Francesca had no wish to disillusion her.

The new home necessitated many visits from its prospective occupants. There were the furnishings to be decided upon, measurements to be made. Francesca had feared Angelo might favour the ornate, when her own inclination was for simplicity, but she found that he had excellent taste. The intimacy of these arrangements often brought the hot colour to her face, especially the choosing of the beds. A double one for the master bedroom—Angelo with a quizzical expression insisted upon that. The twin divans which had caught her fancy, he declared, were 'unfriendly'. A polite way of putting it!

From the front of the house, across the bay, the church tower of the village of Cervo was a striking landmark, especially at night when it was floodlit. Francesca was intrigued by this spot, which stood on a conical hill, and looked almost out of place rising above the urban development surrounding it, but that was a feature of Italy. Amidst the most modern erections, one would come upon a picturesque old alley, usually bedecked with washing, a survival from a much earlier age. Pleased by her interest, Angelo arranged to take her there.

It was, she discovered, a bit of old Italy set among the embellishments of the new. Narrow winding streets and alleyways led up to the summit of the hill, lined with houses which looked so old it seemed impossible that they were still inhabited, which they obviously were. They had been lived in since Roman times, for there were Roman tiles among the masonry.

As at Castel Vecchio, an ancient castle stood behind the church on top of the hill, a building which showed Norman origins, a reminder that the Franks had once overrun the land. Erected upon such steep eminences, these fortified outposts must have been almost impregnable.

The church of San Giovanni Battista crowned the height, its western frontage painted in green and terracotta rising loftily from the steps that gave access to it, though the fabric was flaked and stained with time. Inside was a white marble altar in the shape of a galleon, with tall candles in gilt sticks entwined with living flowers. Cervo had a sad history. A hundred and fifty of its menfolk had gone out to fish for coral to make money for the church and all had been drowned, making the place a village of widows. The altar commemorated their loss.

Angelo and Francesca came out of the church, sobered by the contemplation of this tragedy, and the dim magnificence of the building's interior. They stood together on the top of the semicircle of steps, with the façade of the church soaring up behind them into the limitless blue sky. Before them was a little piazza with a low stone wall dividing it from the drop to the sea, which was visible beyond it, a bright ultramarine expanse, stretching to the horizon. Three alleyways had access to the piazza, the one down which they had come a mere slit between tall umber-coloured houses. To the right, under a succession of arches, was the one they would take, descending steeply into nether gloom. To the left the path continued to ascend, winding between protruding buildings. The wall next to the church was covered with a brilliant mantle of bougainvillea. One solitary umbrella pine stood crooked sentinel beside it, bent at an angle. Sundry pots of gaudy geraniums graced the upward lane. It was a scene typical of old Italy, bathed in sunlight, wrapped in memories of its tempestuous past.

Two barefooted children ran across the piazza to vanish into the labyrinth of passages, and then they were quite alone.

Francesca had taken off her sunglasses upon entering the dusky interior of the church; they dangled from her fingers as she turned impulsively towards Angelo, who seldom wore them. He was looking at her, not at the view, pleased by her enthusiasm.

'It's a fascinating place, Angelo. I think I could learn to love this country of yours.'

He gazed down into her upturned face, the glow in his eyes veiled by his thick eyelashes.

'Could you also learn to love me?'

She caught her breath, startled by the unexpected question. Covertly her eyes slid over his tall, graceful figure, enhanced by the cream slacks and cream knitted shirt he was wearing. The strong light showed blue-black tints in his uncovered hair; his patrician features and strong throat were bronzed by the sun. He was very good to look upon, a true son of the south, vivid as the glowing scene about them, with a hint of hidden ruthlessness, as the thick grey wall under the bougainvillea was a reminder of grim and violent deeds in days gone past, when it had been built to withstand them.

Francesca's heart stirred with an increasing awareness of him, as she answered shakily:

'That ... that wasn't in the bargain.'

'But it could be.' His voice sank to a caressing murmur. 'If the little moon goddess would leave her cold realms to permit herself to be melted by the southern sun.'

She dropped her eyes before the sudden glow in his. The sunlit air was moved by a faint breeze laden with the scent of hidden roses from some concealed garden. Watching her face intently, he said softly:

'It would make our life together ... more harmonious.'

But Francesca would not allow herself to surrender to his magnetism. He was too well versed in seduction. Her compliance was not enough for him, he wanted her to fall in love, and having had too many easy conquests, he expected that she would do so. Instinctively she braced herself to resist him.

'I think too many women have loved you,' she said a

104

little sadly. 'And I don't believe you loved any of them.'

He smiled at this accusation.

'We were not discussing my feelings, but yours.' His voice deepened. 'If I had been among the men who died out there,' he made a gesture towards the sea, 'would you have grieved, Francesca, or would you be relieved to find yourself a rich widow?'

'You're being absurd,' she told him quickly, recoiling from the thought of Angelo dead. It seemed impossible that a being so full of vitality could suddenly be quenched. Yet if he raced cars for a pastime the hazard was very great. Her fertile imagination, stimulated by the story of the widows of Cervo, evoked a vision of a broken body and bleeding flesh. Involuntarily she clutched his arm.

'Angelo, promise me you won't ever race any more.'

He was taken aback. 'Who told you I raced?'

'Everyone knows. Didn't you win the Grand Prix?'

'That was ages ago, past history, *amore mia*, and I have given it up now. Even my sports car has been sold.' He slipped his arm about her waist, drawing her close to him. 'Do you care then about my safety, *cara*?'

She quivered in his hold, her shrinking superseded by something greater. As the sun comes from behind the clouds to illuminate a gloomy landscape, she saw a fair prospect before her, bathed in the light of love. She lifted her face to his, her eyes shining, no longer scared to meet the ardour in his.

'Oh, Angelo!' she murmured.

Voices, loud and shrill, their owners still concealed, broke the slumbrous silence of the piazza, the clatter of advancing footsteps. A tourist party was about to break in upon them. Hastily Angelo removed his arm, and Francesca's moment of vision faded. He made a grimace of distaste as the party came into view. Women clumping along on platform-soled sandals which gave an effect of hooves, perspiring men in the first unbecoming stages of sunburn, unhooking their cameras.

Angelo gave his hand to Francesca to help her down the unbalustraded steps.

'Time we went,' he remarked.

They made their way across to the right-hand archway and into the maze of steep paths beyond. Here they came upon the Oratory of Santa Caterina, which dated from A.D. 1200. It had been the original church before San Giovanni had been built in the seventeenth century.

'This place is very old,' Francesca observed without originality.

'So is a great deal of Liguria beneath the new development.'

Casual remarks. Angelo had withdrawn, deeming the environment too public for further intimate talk, and Francesca was vaguely chilled. She had been on the edge of a great revelation, but the elusive moment had fled before she could grasp its meaning. So had the saints glimpsed paradise, only to have their vision obscured by the press of mundane matters. For a split second she had seen what love could be, but a rush of doubts and misgivings had drowned her perceptions. She distrusted whatever it was Angelo felt for her, and her own feelings were still undefinable.

To disguise her inner disquiet, she chattered gaily about their surroundings, pointing out with amusement a vine with its roots at the pavement edge, its stem snaking up the whole length of a tall house, to display its greenery far above their heads where it reached the light of the sun, for the winding passages were dark and shaded, the close-shuttered houses slightly sinister, coloured grey and brown. The warmth and brilliance of the piazza had been left far behind.

Once or twice Angelo glanced at her with a slightly puzzled expression, but she would not meet his questioning eyes. He concluded that she was regretting the emotion that she had shown on the church steps.

Finally they emerged into the Piazza Victor Emmanuele, an open space on the hill, surrounded by buildings except on the seaward side, nearly level, and crossed by a narrow road.

There was a clump of palm trees in the middle of it, with seats set invitingly beneath them. Tired by climbing so many steps and slopes, Francesca sat down gratefully upon one of them, and Angelo went to fetch her a drink from a bar across the road. This quaint recess in the precipitous side of the hill held the same magic as the one before the church, except that it was a little more populous. Before her, as there, was the line of the sea seen over a low wall, and a sensuous languor crept over her tired limbs.

A woman sitting in a parked car, for cars could reach the piazza, observed her intently, and as Angelo disappeared she got out of the vehicle and came towards her. She was a dark girl, with a plain, large-featured face, and a sulky droop to her mouth, but she had an elegant figure and moved with grace. She seated herself beside Francesca, covertly scrutinising her face and form, and finally she spoke.

'The Signorina Temple, is it not?'

Lost in reverie, her eyes on the deep blue of the sea, her companion's voice recalled Francesca with a start. She turned her head to encounter a pair of dark hostile eyes set deep in a brown-skinned face.

'Yes, I am, but how did you know?' she asked.

'Everyone knows the girl who has bewitched Angelo Vittorini,' the other answered. 'Possibly he has mentioned me—I am Maria Donizetti.'

The name rang a bell, but amid her welter of new impressions Francesca could not recall where she had heard it. Meeting her blank gaze, Maria Donizetti laughed disagreeably.

'Apparently not, yet he should have done so, but then he is a double-dealer. He had promised to marry me.'

'Indeed?' Francesca looked at her in bewilderment. 'I'd no knowledge of a prior attachment.'

'He kept it from you? Of course he had his reasons, now he wants to be off with the old love and on with the new.' She paused, but as Francesca made no comment, she went on in a low voice. 'I think you should know, *signorina*, that he has lived with me.'

One of Angelo's 'episodes' come back from the past to upbraid him supposedly, but it was an unpleasant confrontation, and Francesca was surprised that one as dedicated to beauty as Angelo was, could have found this plain woman attractive, but there was no doubt that she had passion; it was smouldering jealously in her small eyes and the convulsive clasping of her hands. They must have made a fiery combination.

Faintly nauseated, Francesca said:

'I know he has had affairs, but they are over now.'

'Don't you believe it—can the leopard change his spots? You look fastidious, *signorina*, surely you cannot bring yourself to accept my leavings?'

'Meaning you left him? That I doubt, *signorina*.'

The girl's fingers crooked suggestively, Francesca had the impression that she was capable of scratching her face with her long, painted red nails.

'Believe what you please,' she said insolently. 'But this I can tell you—you will find no happiness with him; he does not know what fidelity means.'

Anxious to escape, Francesca looked round and saw to her relief that Angelo was coming towards them carrying two wine glasses on a small round tray.

'*Ciao*, Maria,' he said unconcernedly, as he offered Francesca her drink. 'What brings you to Cervo?'

'Perhaps I wanted to relive memories of other days,' Maria hinted with a sly glance at Francesca. 'Days we have spent together.'

'I was unaware that I had ever been here with you,' Angelo retorted unperturbedly, 'in fact I always understood you to say you disliked the place. But let me introduce my fiancée, Francesca Temple. *Cara*, Maria Donizetti is an old family friend.' He emphasised the word family. 'Would you like a drink, Maria?'

'No, thank you, Angelo,' Maria declined, and all sign of emotion had vanished as she smiled at the man. 'Are you really contemplating getting married?'

Angelo sat down between the two girls, quite at his ease.

Not so Francesca. Brought face to face as she was with a piece of Angelo's past, it was no longer so easy to ignore it. How many more women might she not encounter who would lay claim to past favours? As for the future, she had her own doubts about that. It was very fortunate that she was not in love with him, she told herself fiercely, for otherwise she might suffer if he proved unfaithful. Yet glancing at his fine olive profile, she knew she too could be jealous.

He told Maria calmly, 'More than contemplating. Our wedding day is fixed. Haven't you been invited?'

'My father said something about it, but I could not credit it.' Then she burst out in a spate of Italian, which she did not suspect Francesca could understand. 'It is madness, Angelo, you cannot settle down to matrimony after the life you have led. You may think you can, but I know better. She is very pretty, your Nordic lily, but she is insipid, you will be satiated with her within a week. If you must marry, which I think is a mistake, you have chosen the wrong mate.'

To this tirade, Angelo made no rejoinder, but continued to sip his wine unconcernedly.

Francesca said in Maria's language, 'I've always understood the Italians were a polite people. You are being rude, *signorina*.'

Both her companions stared at her in surprise, and Maria looked momentarily disconcerted. Then she said stiffly:

'I apologise. My deep concern for you both ran away with my tongue, but it is better such truths should be spoken before it is too late.'

'If they are truths,' Angelo told her, 'which they are not.' Anger sounded in his voice. He stood up, looking down at Maria with cold dislike. Watching his face, Francesca felt a qualm. If ever she were unlucky enough to earn his displeasure, she would shrivel before such a look. This was a new facet of his character. She glimpsed in his compressed lips and stony eyes an implacable resentment, which once it was aroused would never forgive.

'You would do well to guard your tongue, Maria,' he went on, 'and mind your own business. Understand that I choose the mate who pleases me, which you do not.' He turned to Francesca. 'Come, *amore mia*,' he said gently.

Leaving the glasses to be collected by the bar attentant, he took her arm possessively and led her away. Glancing over her shoulder, Francesca saw that Maria

Donizetti's face was contorted by jealous rage.

Walking downhill towards the place where he had parked his car, Angelo remarked:

'I did not realise you understood and spoke my language so well.'

'But of course.' She was surprised, but he always talked to her in English. 'After all, my parents have lived here for a long time and Granny used Italian when speaking to me, to make me fluent.'

'Yes, she would, knowing what her plans were,' he agreed with a sidelong glance at her cold profile, for Francesca was remembering where she had seen Maria Donizetti. Of course it had been at the Calvis' dance, where she had appeared as a glamorous oriental, her plain features obscured by a yashmak and a mask.

Angelo did not speak again until they reached the car, remarking as he unlocked it:

'I am sorry that our outing should have been marred by such an unpleasant sequel. I hope you will forget it.'

So he meant to ignore Maria's implications. Looking him straight in the face, Francesca said boldly:

'She told me that she had lived with you.'

'Then she lied,' he returned, 'but she was eaten up with jealousy. A jealous woman will say anything.'

'If she is jealous, you must have given her cause,' Francesca persisted, vaguely needled by his calm dismissal of the other woman's distress. If Maria loved him without hope, he could at least have been kinder to her. 'I suppose she is one of your "episodes"?' Involuntarily a note of sarcasm had sharpened her voice.

He threw up his head with a proud gesture, like a blood horse at the menace of a whip.

'No,' he said emphatically. He opened the door of the car for her. 'Get inside.'

Francesca did not move.

'I wish I could believe you,' she told him.

He made an impatient gesture, then controlling himself, said earnestly: 'Listen, *cara*, I swear to you that I have never been intimate with Maria Donizetti. It is true I have known her off and on for most of my life, because our families are old friends, but beyond that she is nothing to me. She is well connected and extremely wealthy, and my father did suggest that she might be a suitable bride for me, if you proved obdurate. Possibly he has been indiscreet enough to mention the matter to her father, and that has given her ideas, but there was no question of a betrothal. Her hints about Cervo were moonshine. She has an old cousin there she sometimes visits, but I have never taken her there, nor have I had any connection with her beyond the usual social contacts.'

He spoke sincerely and her doubts were lulled.

'Thank you, Angelo,' she said gratefully, getting into the car. As he took his place beside her, she told him reproachfully: 'You could have been a little kinder.'

He laughed shortly. 'The Marias of this world do not understand kindness, they take it as a sign of weakening. A man cannot afford to be weak with a predator.'

Francesca started at the use of that word, one that had more than once occurred to her in regard to Angelo. Two of a kind, she thought, and instantly dismissed the idea as unfair. If Maria were a man-eater, Angelo had not yet shown himself a destroyer.

Dismissing the subject, they chatted impersonally about Cervo during the drive back, but it still lingered in the back of Francesca's mind.

It returned with added force to her when she had

112

gone to bed, and she recalled in detail the events of the Calvis' dance. She saw in her mind's eye a man in the costume of a red devil making his way across the crowded floor to the girl in the oriental dress. He had gone to her as soon as he arrived, drawn as a moth to the candle. Desmond had identified her, one of the richest heiresses on the Riviera.

She had seen them again, dancing together, oblivious of anyone else; she recalled how the girl's body had moulded itself into the man's, as he held her closely, too closely, in the waltz. It had been very much later when she had encountered him in the garden, when the dance was nearly at its end and very likely Maria had gone home. She recollected now that she had not noticed her at the unmasking. Possibly they had left together.

Slowly the conviction grew that he had lied to her about his relations with the girl, and Maria's scathing comment, 'She is insipid, you will be satiated with her within a week,' had been made out of her own knowledge of him. She might be plain, but sexually she could be a flame.

Hitherto, Angelo's past reputation had not caused Francesca any concern. She accepted his assurance that it *was* past, but in the matter of their love affairs men had no scruples about lying to women, and this time she had found him out.

A little wind had risen outside, and moaned softly in the fronds of the palm trees; a cat mewed in pursuit of some amorous quest. Francesca stared bleakly into the darkness, for she was realising that her feelings towards her future husband were changing and she no longer contemplated their union with aversion. During the past few weeks he had made every effort to please her, hoping that she would fall in love with

113

him, for it said little for the art of a practised lover if he could not charm the woman he meant to make his wife. He had been succeeding until she had been brought face to face with the realisation that his attentions were only practised wiles to win a temporary gratification. When he had had his way with her, he would neglect her, reverting to his former habits, Maria had said so, and she must know him very well. He would return to his gambling, his racing, his other women, and she would be marooned in that villa above the sea, eating her heart out in loneliness.

No—never that. Her heart was not yet wholly involved, and she would not permit it to become so. Her budding love for him must be nipped in the bud before it could bloom. She would not allow herself to yearn for a rake and a reprobate. She would steel herself against him, endure what must be endured, and when he tired, let him go without regret. She would have much to compensate her—her parents comfortably settled nearby, Stacey to love and guide, and perhaps her own child. She flushed angrily in the darkness, recalling Angelo's words, 'a man likes to be sure his children are his own'. Her virtue must be unassailable, while he wandered where he would. The eternal difference between the sexes, since to Eve had been given the burden and privilege of producing life.

After all, she had not expected anything more from her marriage, but that day at Cervo she had glimpsed a felicity which might have been hers, until Maria Donizetti had stripped her illusions from her with the cruel reality.

Unfamiliar with strong emotion, a novice at the shrine of love, it did not occur to her that her resolutions were being made much, much too late.

CHAPTER SIX

FRANCESCA TEMPLE and Angelo Giovanni Sebastiano Vittorini were married in the ancient church of San Michele at Castel Vecchio, by special dispensation and with curtailed rites by reason of their different denominations. The ceremony was preceded by the civil marriage and followed by a reception at the Castello, attended by the bride's family and a few intimate friends, among whom were the Donizettis, father and daughter.

To Francesca the whole day was a fantasy, the culmination of weeks of living in a dream. It did not seem to be herself in white dress and veil standing before the altar in the ornate interior of the church. Dimly lit by the stained glass windows in the clerestory, the myriad candles made oases of light. Besides the tall ones on the altar, they were grouped before the statues of the saints in their chapels round the walls and that of the Madonna, illuminating her glittering robes. Frescoes and paintings filled every space, with a plentiful use of gilt. It all added to the total unreality of the scene.

She performed her part mechanically, feeling nothing. She might have been the statue which she ressembled, her face as pale as her clothes; only her hair caught gleams of light, and her eyes were fathomless pools of night. Angelo decked out in formal clothes was least real to her of all, with the beauty of a fallen angel in his classic face. Her fingers were icy cold when they were laid in his, her lips no less so when he gave her a nuptial kiss. She saw concern in his dark eyes,

115

and murmured vaguely:

'It's nothing but nerves,' and glimpsed his reassuring smile.

Nor did she thaw during the brief, formal reception in the great hall of the Castello. Although the day was warm and sunny, the place felt chill, overburdened with its atmosphere of the past. How many brides, willing and unwilling, had been received within its sombre precincts? Francesca wondered. Their last descendant, the Marchese, was as urbane and polished as ever, plying his guests with champagne. Amidst their number, Francesca caught Maria Donizetti's baleful glance.

The newly married couple were not going away. Francesca had pleaded to spend her honeymoon in their new home. Angelo had been granted a week's leave from the business in which he was now taking an active part. She felt it would be less of an ordeal to be there with him in what had now become familiar surroundings than in some strange hotel.

The lights were beginning to sparkle along the waterfronts of the chain of towns along the coast, as he drove her down through the blue dusk to the villa. There they were greeted excitedly by the staff that had been engaged—the chef, Luigi, Angelo's personal man, and various maids. Except for Luigi they did not live in the house, coming in by day, but every one of them was there to greet their master and mistress. They were never treated with the starchy discipline accorded to British servants, and regarded themselves as members of the family.

'A shower and a change, I think,' Angelo decreed, when at last they were alone. 'I will be glad to get out of these ridiculous clothes.'

Francesca had already discarded her bridal white for

116

a plain blue dress and thin coat. She shed the latter in her bedroom, realising that it was no longer hers alone. Though Angelo had a dressing-room next to it, his belongings were already impinging upon her privacy. He had dropped his jacket upon the bed, pulled off his tie and thrown it on the dressing-table. She wondered vaguely if he were untidy in his ways.

The telephone connection beside the bed shrilled loudly. Automatically she raised the receiver, and her ear was met with a spatter of excited Italian.

'Angelo,' she called, 'please come. It seems something has happened to your father.'

He came at once out of the bathroom, water glistening on his dark hair, a towel hastily wrapped about his body. She eyed his brown torso with a quickening of her heartbeats. He was superbly muscled and smooth as a bronze statue.

He took the instrument from her hand and listened, his brow creasing in concern. Francesca moved away, while he seemed to be expostulating with the caller. Finally he said resignedly:

'*Si*, I will come.' He cradled the instrument and looked at her ruefully. 'He has had a fall. They do not seem to know the extent of the damage. I am afraid I shall have to leave you.'

She lowered her eyelids hastily, but not before he had seen the flash of relief in her eyes.

'Too bad,' she murmured mechanically, adding quickly: 'Is it serious?'

'Maybe,' he said shortly. He was collecting his clothes. 'I may be away all night. It is some way to the Castello.'

He went back into the bathroom leaving the door ajar, as he continued to speak to her. 'You had better go to bed, *cara mia*. I will return as soon as I can.' An

117

edge crept into his voice. 'Though perhaps you will not be too impatient for my coming.'

Ignoring this thrust, she said inadequately: 'I'm so sorry.'

'For him, or for me? What a thing to happen on our wedding night! I wonder if it is really essential that I go.'

'Of course you must go, there isn't anyone else.'

'True enough, and the servants seem to be running round in circles.'

He came back, having hurriedly donned slacks and a sweater. '*Arrivederci, amore mia,*' he said softly, and drew her into his arms.

'You'll give me a ring?' she suggested. 'I'd like to know how he is.'

'Yes, in about a couple of hours,' He glanced round the room, the inviting bed, the slim girl in his arms with her loosened web of hair, her eyes dark and watchful. '*Dio,*' he muttered, 'it is hard to go.'

'But you will be back as soon as you can?'

'You bet I will!'

His kiss was long and close. Then he thrust her from him almost roughly, and went out of the door. Francesca heard his footsteps running down the steps, his impatient voice calling for his man. She sat down upon the bed with a feeling of anticlimax. She had been keyed up to meet the demands of the night, and now she had been reprieved. She heard the car going down the drive, Angelo was driving recklessly fast. An apprehensive chill crept over her—suppose he had an accident, did not come back? He was in no mood to take care. Then she might be free of him for ever, but she did not want freedom at such a price. It came to her then that his loss would leave a great gap in her life.

Luigi knocked on the door and she bade him enter.

'*Scusi, signora*, but the master said to tidy up.' He glanced round at the signs of Angelo's hurried departure. 'Should I come back later?'

'No, I was just going.'

She left the room quickly, aware of the man's sympathetic gaze. To him the deprivation of her husband on her wedding night was a major tragedy.

She went into the *salotto* and its quiet tore at her nerves. She could not bear to sit there alone waiting in her emotional state. Angelo had said it would be two hours before he could ring. She looked out of the window at the lights of the town, which seemed to invite her. She would go out, walk off her restlessness among the gay crowds along the waterfront. It was not far down to the promenade, she could be there in a few moments. She went to the door and called Luigi.

'I'm going out for a little while. I won't be gone long.'

He looked astonished and began to expostulate.

'Only a stroll,' she interrupted quickly. 'I will be all right.'

He shrugged his shoulders eloquently. Of course she was a foreigner, but even so, it was a strange thing to do, and he felt responsible for her.

'I'm only going a little way,' she insisted. 'No harm can come to me. I'll be back before Signor Vittorini rings.'

A quarter of a mile of twisting road led down into the town. Cars passed her in quick succession going up and down. She kept in close to the bank, there was no pavement, thinking that if she were knocked down it would be one way out of her difficulties. It would be a hospital bed for her and not a marriage bed, she thought wryly, but she did not deliberately court an accident.

The road came out between lighted hotels and she made her way on to the wide promenade. A stone balustrade was between her and the sea, faintly luminous under the stars. Palm trees stood in serried ranks between her and the road, their tall trunks smoothly shaved, illuminated by the lights, their crown of long fronds lost in the shadows above. Tables and chairs were set out along the further edge of the promenade, where couples, many of them elderly tourists, mums and dads who had come south for a long anticipated vacation in the sun, were enjoying a last drink in peace and quiet. The younger people preferred the night clubs or the brightly lit interiors of the bars.

Francesca walked along, unaware of the masculine eyes which followed her. She was not afraid of being accosted, feeling that she could deal effectively with any impudent Romeo, and her mind was upon other things. Nevertheless when a man stepped in front of her she halted in some alarm, until she saw with astonishment that he was English and she knew him.

'Fran!' Desmond exclaimed.

'Oh, Des!' She held out both her hands to him, his desertion forgotten in the joy of seeing a familiar face. He drew her towards him and kissed her.

'What luck meeting you!'

'But . . . but how do you come to be here?'

'I had an assignment covering a conference that's being held here. I've been up to Bellavista and found the house shut up. Fran darling, I've been nearly off my head with worry wondering what happened to you. Have you solved your difficulties?'

That reminded her. She withdrew her hands, saying coldly:

'Your concern is a little surprising after the way you left me in the lurch.'

'I couldn't help it, it wasn't my doing.'

'Really?'

'Yes, really. Fran, I want to explain. It was a rotten shame. Let's sit down and have a drink while I tell you about it.'

She had always been puzzled by that enigmatical note which he had left for her, and now he was proposing to enlighten her, but if there was an exonerating explanation, it had come much too late.

She allowed him to lead her to where an awning formed an open-air café facing the sea. It was furnished with upholstered swinging loungers, and she sank down upon one of them with a sigh.

'It's nice to see you, Des.'

He was a bit of her old life, her own countryman, and he had been her friend. Why, oh, why had he left her? Between them they could have worked out an answer to her problems.

A waiter came to take their order, and she asked for coffee. When he had gone back across the street to fetch it, Desmond said:

'What happened, Fran? Did you make out all right?'

Francesca smiled wryly. 'Quite all right, but before I tell you what occurred, I'd like to know why you ran away.'

He looked slightly shamefaced.

'I couldn't help it, Fran. That brute from the Castello—didn't you tell me it was nicknamed Diavolo, and never was a place better called—threatened me. He told me to get out, or else ... and for all I knew he might have had a band of thugs ready to dispose of me. I was forced to go.'

She stared at him incredulously, not believing this unlikely tale.

'At first I thought you'd put him up to it,' Desmond went on. 'You'd told me he wanted to marry you, and he had all the answers for that tiresome family of yours. But when I got away, I thought about it, and I was sure I'd misjudged you. You're incapable of double dealing. I worried about you and when this chance came to get back here, I was delighted.'

'You could have written,' she pointed out.

He hesitated. 'Well ... er ... as a matter of fact I did, but you didn't answer. Perhaps you didn't get it?'

She shook her head.

He said more confidently: 'It must have been intercepted. I wouldn't put it past him.'

The waiter returned with their coffee, and Francesca stirred hers meditatively, her mind in a whirl. Could Desmond's preposterous story be true? She remembered the black car speeding away from the house —Angelo's car, he had driven Desmond away himself, wanting her to believe he had deserted her. She knew there was a ruthless streak in her husband, and he would stick at nothing to obtain his own ends. But he had no right to interfere between herself and Desmond, it was an unwarrantable piece of arrogance, and one she could not lightly forgive. It was partly pique at Desmond's defection which had led to her consent to becoming engaged to Angelo. He had counted upon that, he knew women too well, but this time he had overreached himself. She could never condone such an action.

But Desmond's part in that night's proceedings had hardly been a heroic one. She said gently:

'He couldn't have harmed you, Des.'

'Oh, couldn't he! He looked like a devil, and I don't

doubt that sinister-looking castle of his is full of villains. We hear things in the news, you know, about these Italians and the Mafia and what not. I shouldn't be surprised if he were in with that lot. I didn't want to be found on those hills with my body riddled with bullets.'

He was afraid she would think he had been cowardly, and was laying it on thick to excuse himself. He owed Angelo a grudge for intimidating him and depriving him of his girl, and his light eyes flickered with triumphant malice, as he saw a chance of revenge.

Francesca shivered at his words; there might be some truth in them; though she did not believe it possible that Angelo would commit murder to remove an inconvenient rival, he might have had Desmond beaten up. Thinking of the danger he had faced upon her account, she laid her hand on his sleeve, murmuring:

'I don't blame you, Des, it must have been a horrid situation, but I can't quite believe Angelo would threaten violence.'

'Oh, you know what these Latin types are when their passions are aroused,' he said airily, and Francesca quailed, for that she was about to learn. He looked at her beseechingly: 'I still love you, Fran. I know I forgot myself that night, but you don't know how tantalising you are.'

His eyes became greedy as they travelled over her. He had forgotten how enchanting she was, and this chance meeting had revived all his desire for her. That gilded hair, her eyes which looked so dark until a man looked into them and discovered they were violets. The blue dress she was wearing was beautifully cut, and moulded to her figure, she had always had style, and her inaccessibility was an added charm, the virginal air that clung to her, was a challenge and a provocation.

'I'll never offend again,' he went on. 'I'll wait patiently until you're ready to marry me, and I've had a rise, I can help with your family now.'

Francesca covered her face with her hands.

'You're too late, Des. I was married to Angelo today.'

'Fran, no! You can't be.'

'But I am. I was more or less coerced into it, and I thought you wouldn't come back.'

Briefly she related the events which had led up to it, and the reason why she was alone tonight. But when she came to the Marchese's accident and Angelo's precipitate departure, he looked at her oddly.

'That's strange, because I saw him, and there was a woman beside him. They had to slow down behind a truck, and I was walking down, so I had a good look at them. It was that plain girl, what's her name, we saw her at the dance, and he didn't look like a bridegroom who'd been torn from his bride.'

Maria Donizetti. Francesca recalled her venomous glances at the reception. But how had she linked up with Angelo? It had not been her voice on the telephone. That message, she was certain, was genuine.

'Are you sure it was Angelo?' she asked.

'Couldn't mistake him, I'd never forget that face. Darling, I'm sorry if I've upset you, perhaps there's some explanation.' But he sounded as if he thought that was extremely unlikely.

Francesca stared blindly at the sea.

'What am I going to do?' she whispered.

This was a betrayal of the worst kind. On her wedding day her husband had left her to pick up his former love. Perhaps he was only giving Maria a lift if she were going his way, but he had left in such haste, that it seemed strange he would stop to take on a passenger. It was an ominous incident in the light of her deep distrust of those two.

Desmond took her hand in his.

'It seems I've met you in the nick of time,' he said urgently. 'Come away with me now, Fran, before he gets back. If you haven't—you know—slept with him, we can get this marriage annulled. I'll take you back to England and we'll forget we ever got mixed up with this Italian desperado.'

She thought wistfully of England, its grey mists and green fields, the security it offered, and shook her head.

'I can't, Des. I owe the Vittorinis too much. Oh, if it were only myself,' she burst out wildly, 'I'd come with you like a shot, but I don't know what would happen to the others.'

'I expect they'd manage somehow. Why must you be made a victim, Fran?'

She smiled wanly. 'I expect I've too great a sense of family responsibility, but I made a bargain with Angelo, and I must do my part.'

'You needn't keep faith with a deceiver and a liar, Fran, for he lied to you about me. And I thought you loved me, don't I count at all with you?'

'You know you do. Oh, if only you'd come sooner, if I'd known what really happened!'

He moved impatiently. 'It's no good regretting the might-have-been.' He looked at her shrewdly. 'Are you sure you haven't fallen for this ruffian?'

Francesca started. 'Good heavens no! I'd as soon fall for Lucifer himself, and nothing you've told me tonight is to his credit.'

She fell silent, considering, playing with her coffee spoon, while Desmond watched her anxiously.

Angelo's melodramatic threat to Desmond had been

a mean and despicable means to discredit him in her eyes by forcing him to desert her. Possibly Desmond might have put up a better show instead of slinking off, but Angelo had been on his own territory, and Desmond was not to know what powers he might possess. Whether his letter of explanation had really been intercepted or had merely gone astray she did not know, but it was possible. That Angelo was having a secret affair with Maria was also possible; he had already lied to her about his connection with that lady.

Underlying all her rising resentment against him lay the fear of him, which she had never managed to entirely subdue, and which Desmond's story had increased. She had always shrunk from the ruthless element which she had sensed in him. That that was her main reason for wanting to escape, she would not acknowledge, even to herself; she preferred to magnify his deceit and arrogance. Desmond's plan was a very real temptation.

As for her family, her father was doing well in his new position. She did not think the Vittorinis would be so petty as to deprive him of it now that he had proved his worth, merely to spite her. If she went to England, she could send for Stacey as soon as she was established. She need have no compunction about leaving Angelo. He had driven away her lover with threats at the time when she had needed his support most, which was inexcusable, and not even for love of her but because his father desired possession of a plot of land. She was reminded of the Biblical story of Naboth's vineyard. Murder was done to obtain that. Angelo had threatened murder, or near murder, to get Bellavista, before he knew it would be coming on the market. Jezebel had had Naboth stoned to give Ahab his desire, and there was something medieval about the set-up at Castel Vecchio which made such conduct credible.

Yet when she had told him he need not marry her to gain the property, he had persisted—why? He had said he had a fancy for pale gold hair—a sudden infatuation, she supposed, but infatuations can die as quickly as they are born, and already he was regretting Maria.

She said quietly: 'If I come with you, Des, there'll be a long delay before we can get married waiting for this marriage to be annulled. Are you sure you're prepared to wait?'

Unless Angelo, incensed by her behaviour, hastened the proceedings, which he might well do so that he could put Maria Donizetti in her place.

Desmond saw that she was weakening and triumph swelled in his breast. He envied Angelo his wealth and his good looks, and he had stolen his girl, but in spite of all his assets, she was coming back to him.

'I've told you I'll wait,' he said firmly.

She glanced at her watch; Angelo's two hours were nearly up, and he would be ringing the villa. She shivered, thinking of what awaited her when he returned.

'Oh, Des, this place has never seemed like home; the sunshine is too bright. I'm longing to see England again. Take me back!'

She extended her hand to him and he clasped it fervently, though he would have been better pleased if she had said she was longing for him.

'I'll take you, but you must go back and get your passport and change into something less conspicuous. Luckily my conference broke up tonight. My car is hired, but I can leave it in Genoa. We'll get a flight from there. When do you expect this man to come home?'

She stood up. 'Not for ages, it's a long way from

Castel Vecchio. He mayn't come back at all tonight, but I'd better hurry.'

Desmond drove her up the hill, but she refused to let him come in with her. Luigi would be on the look-out for her and the other servants might be around.

'I'll tell him I'm going to bed,' she said, 'then I'll creep out at the back. You'd better wait at the bottom of the hill.'

He laughed exultantly. 'A real elopement, darling. Thank God I was in time!'

Her first question as she re-entered the house was to ask the hovering Luigi whether Angelo had rung up. He had not done so. A sudden suspicion came into her mind. Was the whole thing a put-up job? Had Maria summoned him, even on his wedding day, and he was not at Castel Vecchio at all, but with her? Over-wrought and over-excited, she was ready to credit this most unlikely supposition. She wanted to credit it, it would excuse her flight.

Luigi was looking at her with concern. He attrib-uted her agitation to more obvious causes. Kindly he advised her to go to bed and take a sedative. His master was sure to be back by morning, and—he smiled slyly—there was always tomorrow night.

She bade him *buona notte*, told him not to sit up and went to her room. Tomorrow night she would be in England.

Yet when she went into her bedroom, she was aware of a curious reluctance to leave. Angelo had been very good to her. On her toilet table the silver-backed brushes, the expensive scent from the perfumery at Grasse, the embroidered robe hanging on the door, were evidence of his generosity. Bribes, she thought scornfully, to reconcile me to my lot, and tried to whip up indignation against him for cold-bloodedly parting her from her lover, but it no longer seemed such a heinous offence. She recalled almost wistfully his last kiss ... but he's with Maria, she told herself fiercely. The other girl had probably gone with him to the Castello.

She took out of a drawer a pair of slacks and a light sweater which would be unnoticeable among so many others similarly clad. Her passport, which she could not at first locate, was strictly speaking invalid, but it would not be questioned at this point, though Angelo might of course ring up the airport. She did not think this was likely, he would be too angered by her desertion to want to search for her. Besides, with luck, she would be on her way before he returned.

She put the bare essentials, nightdress and toothbrush, into a large shoulder bag with her purse and her loose cash. She still had a little left in the bank, a British bank, to tide her over.

She walked to the door and looked back at the wide bed with its silken coverlet. That at least she would be spared. She switched out the light and went into the passage, wondering if it would be safe to go out of the front door, or to creep through the servants' quarters as she had suggested to Desmond, but Luigi might still be up and around, so it had better be the front. She groped her way to the door to check with a leap of her heart, as it opened to disclose a dark figure against the starshine outside. Then the passage was flooded with light and her blood ran cold as she saw Angelo standing before her.

'It was all a bit unnecessary,' he told her. 'My father fell and broke his wrist. When I arrived he had been made comfortable and swore at me for coming on such a night. I did not stop to ring you but came straight back. I have been driving like the devil...' He broke off, becoming aware of her dress, the bag hanging from her shoulders. 'What is this?' he rasped. 'A masquerade?'

'No. I'm going out.'

'At this hour of the night?'

'Yes. Unfortunately you've returned too soon. I meant to be far away when you came back.' She met his suspicious gaze calmly. 'You promised to let me go if I found I couldn't go through with it. I've decided that I can't.'

'It is too late for you to change now,' he told her. Unexpectedly he lunged forward, whisking the bag from her shoulders, and spilling its telltale contents on to the floor. 'A midnight flitting! Might one ask if you're going alone?' Suave, almost gently put, but in his eyes a deadly menace.

She hesitated, decided frankness was best and told him defiantly:

'I'm going with Desmond, he's here in Liguria. He's told me how you threatened him if he didn't get out just when I needed him most. That was a rotten thing to do, Angelo.'

'Believe me, he didn't need much persuading,' he said drily. 'The prospect of being burdened with your responsibilities was more intimidating than any threat I could offer.'

'Of course you'd say that, but it isn't true. I ... I loved Desmond,' unconsciously she used the past tense. 'I'd never have agreed to marry you if I hadn't believed he'd deserted me.'

A slight sound betrayed that Luigi was listening. Angelo pushed her unceremoniously into the *salotto*, leaving her bag and its contents for the man to pick up.

'Now,' he began, standing with his back against the

door, 'get this straight. That lily-livered specimen needed no urging to desert you...'

'Then you did threaten him?'

'I merely pointed out that there were healthier spots than Castel Vecchio. *Dio mio*, Francesca, do you imagine any threat, however violent, would have driven me away from the woman I loved? A woman, moreover, who was in dire distress?'

'I've no idea what you would do in similar circumstances,' she told him scornfully, 'and I don't believe you've ever loved a woman. What you feel for my sex is something quite different.'

'I am not going to split hairs over that. What I feel is very satisfactory—to me. Your ideas are culled from cheap romances, it is time you faced realities.'

She said nothing, though her lips quivered.

'I wonder that young reprobate had the nerve to return,' he went on bitingly. 'Was he hoping your family had been disposed of and you were no longer encumbered?'

'He came here on an assignment and we met accidentally. He'd been up to Bellavista and was worried about what had become of me.'

'Indeed? He'd waited a long time to contact you.'

'He told me he had written, but I never got the letter.'

Angelo laughed unpleasantly. 'My dear, don't be so naïve. Of course there never was any letter.' He looked her up and down. 'Had you no compunction about breaking our pact? I have fulfilled my part of it, Francesca.'

'It's null and void, because you cheated,' she cried fiercely. 'And what's more, when you left here this evening, you were with Maria Donizetti, and you needn't deny it, because you were seen. Why don't you go back to her and leave me alone?'

'Because I have no wish to do so. As for this evening, I found her by the roadside, her car having broken down, and an urgent engagement awaiting her in Imperia. Would you have me be discourteous to a family friend, a woman in difficulties, because I have married a wife?'

She was silent, knowing his explanation was feasible, though it was strange that he had found time to succour Maria when he was in such a hurry.

'I repeat,' he went on, 'I have married a wife and I cannot forget the vows we made together this morning, if you can. You will not leave me, Francesca.'

She said intensely: 'Is it nothing to you that I love another man's little finger more than your whole body?'

It was quite untrue, but she wanted to wound him, to break through the mask of cool restraint that he was wearing, a mask that concealed—what?

'Nothing at all,' he returned imperturbably. 'And I think you are deceiving yourself. However, since you mention bodies, it is yours I want, and I have paid a heavy price for it. I refuse to be cheated. You will take off those ridiculous clothes and go to bed. I will come to you later.'

More than once Francesca had likened him to Lucifer, and he looked satanic now, with his black brows knitted over his glittering eyes, the only live things in the marble immobility of his face. She shrank from him with the look of a trapped hare.

'No,' she breathed. 'Oh, please—no!'

He went to the sideboard, taking out of the cupboard beneath it a bottle and glasses. 'This may help,' he told her.

'You think that if you make me drunk...'

'It will be easier for you,' he said almost kindly.

She sat down, feeling her legs would no longer sustain her, while he poured out the wine. When he handed her a full glass, she gulped it down eagerly. Perhaps he was right; if her mind was blurred, she might forget her fear. He refilled her glass and sat down opposite to her, lighting a cheroot. He looked to her excited fancy like a hawk waiting to swoop upon its prey. Unable to bear the increasing tension, she broke into speech, endeavouring to keep her voice steady and reasonable.

'You're making a big mistake, Angelo, by keeping me here, and I made a mistake by agreeing to marry you. But if you let me go now, it can be remedied by an annulment. You will be free to marry Maria Donizetti, who I'm sure, in spite of your denials, would suit you much better than I would. I'm grateful for what you've done for me and mine, but once I've got a job, I can take Stacey to live with me, and ...' Her voice died away under his quizzical regard.

'You are being childish,' he returned. 'If I wanted to marry Maria I would have done so long ago, and it is much too late to talk about making mistakes. You were not forced to marry me, but you agreed to do so. Today I gave you my name,' he lifted his head proudly, 'a name that has meant something in the past, and I will have no gossip attached to it. Tonight I intend to make you my wife in fact as well as name. Your obsession with that singularly uninteresting young man is no compliment to me, and the best way to drive him out of your thoughts is to give you something else to think about.'

His anger seemed to have faded, and the smile he gave her was almost tender.

Refusing to be melted, she whispered intensely:

'Even though you'll make me hate you?'

He shrugged his shoulders. 'Neither love nor hate have much to do with this very ordinary experience. I shall be very gentle with you, but I see nothing to be gained by procrastination, in fact the sooner you assume your marital duties the better it will be for you—you will discover that they are not really so terrifying. I had hoped for a very different state of affairs, but...' He shrugged his shoulders again and looked at her searchingly. 'You seem to have built up a picture of me as some sort of diabolical being who wants to rape you. Perhaps it is partly my fault for first making a pass at you in the disguise of the Devil. I notice you are very impressionable.' His mouth twisted humorously. 'I am only a man, *cara*, and human, and will not scorch you with fire and brimstone, though from your expression you look as though you expected it. But...' his voice became stern, 'I will stand no more nonsense about this Desmond person. You are my wife and you will please forget him as quickly as possible.'

Overcome by wine and conflicting emotions, Francesca let this long speech wash over her, barely taking in the import of his words, his suave, quiet delivery acting as a soporific, but the last sentence roused her.

'I can't do that,' she said defiantly. 'Memories of love can't be forgotten to order.'

A flash of anger crossed his face, to be instantly suppressed.

'Then at least have the decency to keep your unfaithful yearnings to yourself,' he said coldly.

In the ensuing silence, Francesca's heartbeats seemed to be suffocating her. With shaking fingers, she raised her wine glass and drained it.

Angelo stubbed out the end of his cheroot and rose from his chair, and came towards her, holding out his hands. A singularly sweet smile changed the severity of his face.

'Come, *amore mia*,' he said softly.

Francesca threw up her chin. 'I'm not a child to be scolded one moment and coaxed the next!'

'You are very much a child, *cara*. Come, I am only going to teach you how to love.'

'You're the last person ever to do that,' she flashed, and laughed hysterically. 'What do you know of love? I'd sooner be mauled by a fiend—in fact I think you are one!'

He flinched as if she had struck him, and suddenly she knew that she had done just that. He stood looking at her bleakly, while his face hardened to granite and his mouth set in a grim line.

'I will never forgive you for saying that,' he told her with a quietness far more deadly than any vituperation. 'And since you prefer the hard way, the hard way it shall be.'

There was no gentleness in the iron grip of the hands which pulled her out of her seat, no tenderness in the arms that enclosed her body like steel bands as he lifted her. He carried her into the bedroom and flung her down upon the bed. Then he shut and locked the door.

bitterness crept into Maria's voice. She had had some bad moments of

CHAPTER SEVEN

FROM that night onwards, Angelo became a stranger to his wife, moreover he seemed changed, older, quieter, and the gaiety that had once been his had vanished. He rose early, before Francesca was up, returning for dinner and not always then. In the evenings he either shut himself away from her, saying he had work to do, or went out. He never told her what he was doing or where he was going. If she questioned him, she received polite evasive answers, so that she soon ceased to do so. Nor did he ever ask her how she spent her time. He was always unfailingly courteous to her, but his total lack of interest in her pursuits was only too painfully apparent.

Though he never referred to the events of their wedding night, she knew that he would never forget or forgive her part in them. That implacable resentment which she had glimpsed at Cervo when he had reprimanded Maria was now fully directed against herself. Only by the most abject submission had she any hope of breaking it down, and that she was too proud to attempt, especially as she was doubtful if she would succeed. Only if he loved her would he ever forgive her, and it became more and more obvious that he had no sentiment for her at all. She was his wife, an ornament to his house, that he liked to see beautifully groomed and turned out, but in whose heart and mind he took no interest. They were like two mere acquaintances, compelled to share one roof, and hopelessly estranged.

Except for those nights when he came to her, nights which she tried to forget during the daylight hours, for he could rouse her to a passionate response, of which she was vaguely ashamed since it was not sanctified by love. On the purely physical plane they were attune, and when waking in the morning after the heavy sleep of exhaustion, she would turn towards where he had lain, unable to believe that there could be no tender aftermath, she would find him gone, and when she appeared for breakfast Luigi would inform her that the master had left early for the factory. Then the bitter realisation would wash over her that she was only a means to an end. He wanted a son.

So did she. A child might draw them together. Although he had no love for his wife, only the natural desire for a beautiful woman, he would revere the mother of his son. Planning for him would break down the barrier of hurt pride that Angelo had erected between them, and she dreamed dreams of the time when they would become a united happy family. Francesca had to admit that she was no longer indifferent to her husband, she doubted if she had ever really been so, he had always fascinated her, and now he was inaccessible, her yearning to be friends increased. Though he was at times her lover, she derived no real satisfaction from a relationship that left their spirits far apart. Often she wondered if she could not do something to soften him, but whenever she tried to make an advance, her overture was met with a cold surprise, and a faint contemptuous smile, so that she was forced to the conclusion that any demonstration of affection from her was unwelcome. She too had her share of pride and took refuge in a chill disdain.

What had happened to Desmond she did not know nor did she greatly care. She had come to the conclusion that his version of what had occurred between himself and Angelo had been much exaggerated, if not actually untrue. Angelo had probably suggested that he had better go away, but he would never have implemented his threat. It had been a test of the young man's courage, which had failed lamentably. Francesca surmised that while he had waited for her, he had seen Angelo's car arrive and had beaten a hasty retreat. He belonged to a past that had become infinitely remote and she rarely gave him a thought.

Angelo placed no restrictions upon her comings and goings, confident now that she would not attempt to leave him. She had her own car and a lavish dress allowance. She appeared to be a spoiled and indulged bride and was the envy of all their acquaintances; only she knew the hollowness beneath the outward show.

Stacey was often with her, for the convent celebrated many saints' days which were holidays. These the child much preferred to spend with her sister than with her parents. Bruno, at her request, was brought down to the villa, with occasional disastrous effects on the flower beds, when he slipped his tether. He was actually getting on in years, and did not mind restricted liberty, so long as he had plenty of food and shelter.

In Stacey's presence Angelo would become his old self again, gay, tenderly teasing and eager to indulge the child with treats and presents. Watching them together, Francesca could visualize how he would be with his own children, but would she still be excluded when they came? He made no attempt to draw her into his intimacy with Stacey, but surely he would relax and forgive her, once she became a mother? But of that there was as yet no sign.

Stacey had already benefited from the change. Neatly dressed and well groomed, she showed signs of becoming an exceptionally beautiful girl, and her manners were vastly improved.

'Am I becoming the sort of sister you want me to be?' she asked Angelo anxiously, and he replied promptly:

'You are already so. I am proud to be seen about with you,' and suggested a run out to Alassio, and a boat trip to Isola Gallinara, the small island off its coast, so called because the Romans kept chickens there, it being a day when he too had a holiday.

He did not include Francesca in his plans, and it was only at Stacey's urging that he reluctantly asked if she would like to come with them.

She refused, pleading that sea trips made her feel ill, knowing he wanted to be alone with the child, but it was with a heavy heart that she watched them set out together, Stacey proud to be in the front seat of his car, chattering volubly, and Angelo laughing at her sallies. He never laughed when he was alone with her.

Since they were both fond of her, Stacey was the one subject which Angelo occasionally discussed with her.

'She shows a talent for drawing,' Francesca said one night at dinner, after a visit from her sister. 'She might go to an art school later on and be trained for commercial art, I believe it's possible to make a living at that.'

'She has no need to earn a living,' Angelo returned. 'With that face she will not be single long. The important thing will be to find her a husband.'

'Which you will expect to select for her? I fancy Stacey will want to choose her own.'

'Provided she meets the right people, it should be possible to combine suitability with inclination,' he told her. 'I myself will give her a dowry.'

Generous to a fault, and once he had made a similar observation about himself and her, and how wrong he had been.

'You think that's all a woman is good for, don't you?' she said accusingly. 'Husband, home and children,' and saw the slight contraction of his facial muscles on the last word.

'I do,' he admitted, 'and I hope ere long...' He glanced at her and sighed. 'A woman is incomplete without a child.'

'And so far I have failed to complete my destiny?'

'I did not mean to reproach you, it is as God wills,' he returned piously, and turned his attention to his wine.

Francesca watched him pour the ruby liquid from the cut glass decanter into his glass, the appreciative way he savoured its bouquet before he drank. His suave olive face was an effective mask for his true feelings, which she could never gauge, his incredibly long lashes swept his cheeks. He was dressed formally as he was going to some entertainment that night. Linen and black jacket were immaculate. Luigi looked after his clothes, and Francesca was never allowed to touch them. How different life would have been with a man like Desmond, she mused, when she would have had to perform all the intimate domestic duties from which she was here excluded. Even the kitchen was ruled by an efficient chef, and all she was expected to do was to look decorative. Decorative she was—her silk dinner dress in heavy crêpe had come from a Milanese couture house, her hair had been dressed by an expensive coiffeur, a diamond pendant sparkled round her neck and diamonds glittered on her fingers. Even when they were alone Angelo insisted that she must dress to do him credit. Occasionally he brought back unexpected guests to dinner, and she had to be prepared for every eventuality.

It was all this affluence that helped to maintain the

barrier between them. If they had had only moderate means, if she had had to cook and clean for him, perform the little personal services which were the duties of a normal wife, there might have been some chance of breaking it down. The minor catastrophes of domesticity would be something over which they could lament and laugh together, but none occurred in that well-run establishment, or if they did, they were concealed from its master.

Thinking along these lines, her face softened from the grave reserve which was becoming habitual to her, the curves of her lips relaxed and her eyes became luminous. Watching her from across the table, Angelo drew a quick breath, but all he said was:

'You do not agree with my ideas?'

'Er ... what? I'm afraid my thoughts have wandered.'

'Along pleasant lines, evidently.'

'Not particularly. I was wondering how you would react if I had to darn your socks and launder your smalls.'

'What an extraordinary train of thought! You should be thankful you do not have to perform such menial tasks.'

'It would be something to do.' With her elbows on the table she linked her hands, resting her chin upon the platform they formed, while she considered the man opposite to her. 'I might even enjoy doing things like that . . for you.'

He ignored the wistful note in her voice, staring at her incredulously. 'You have bourgeois leanings,' he said contemptuously, 'which are belied by your appearance.' A gleam came into his eyes. 'You do for me the most important thing of all.'

'Oh, that!' She transferred her hands to her lap and sighed. 'I don't flatter myself I'm the only one who serves you so.'

His face froze. 'You never have had a very high opinion of my moral character, have you?' he said accusingly. 'Though all your deductions are merely founded on hearsay.'

'What else have I to go upon?' she asked reproachfully.

'There is such a thing as trust,' he suggested. 'But in my case I know my appearance and my nationality are against me.'

'Oh, Angelo...' she began desperately, and paused, trying to find the right words to appeal to him. Blind trust was a lot to expect when he never confided in her.

'*Basta*,' he said shortly. 'I do not want any protestations, since I doubt their sincerity.'

Stabbed by this cruel utterance, but concealing her wound, she asked pointedly:

'Then may I ask where you are going tonight and with whom?'

'Certainly. I am going to the casino at San Remo, and I am going alone.'

So he was gambling again.

'You're reverting to your bad old ways?' she said lightly.

He shrugged his shoulders. 'I work hard. I need some distraction occasionally.'

'Which you can't find at home?'

He compressed his lips. 'You do not attempt to amuse me.'

'What do you want me to do?' she enquired mockingly. 'Dance for you, play, sing perhaps? I'm afraid my education neglected the tricks of the harem.'

He smiled sardonically. 'I can hire experts to do all that, but I find no pleasure in the society of one who regards my presence as something that has to be endured.'

'I don't know why you should think that,' she began, but he held up his hand to check her.

'It is obvious, and you need not manufacture excuses, they cannot gloss over the hard words that have passed between us. I have a long memory, Francesca.'

'You certainly have,' she cried bitterly. 'But there were other times...' She thought of Cervo, when he had shown something approaching tenderness, the reassuring smile that he had given her in church on their wedding day.

'I cannot recall them,' he said coldly.

Needled, she said angrily: 'I wonder you bother to come home at all.'

'The reason again is obvious.' He looked at her thoughtfully. 'Perhaps this antipathy between us is what is preventing the desired issue.'

She wanted to cry out that it was all his doing, she felt no antipathy towards him, but the aloof expression on his face restrained her. She could not get through to him, and he would only snub her. She wondered if he actually disliked her. Pained beyond endurance by that thought, she said sadly:

'Our marriage is hardly working out, is it? Wouldn't it be better to let me go and find yourself someone more compatible? I'm not happy, and I don't think you are. We would be better apart.'

He sighed. 'Possibly, but the fact remains that I married you. After all, it is early days yet and in time you may become more reconciled to your life here. It will be better if and when...' Suspicion flashed into his face, and his eyes became keen and penetrating as they bored into hers. 'You are not trying to thwart me in that respect, are you?'

She stared back perplexed, and then as his meaning dawned, flamed scarlet.

'How dare you suggest such a thing? I want children as much as you do.'

'Do you?' He seemed to doubt her assertion, and added harshly: 'I've known women do unpardonable things out of spite.'

She put her hand over her mouth to conceal her trembling lips. He was cruel to misjudge her so, and he would not allow her to defend herself. If he could attribute such motives to her, he must hate her.

Since the meal was concluded, he lit one of his favourite cheroots and stood up. He looked down at her bent fair head with an unfathomable expression. The artificial light gilded the coiled masses of her hair; it had grown much longer and she wore it swept up on to her small head, deeming the style more suited to her new status. The nape of her neck gleamed like ivory, encircled by the gold chain of her pendant. Thin chiffon sleeves covered her slim arms. She still had that aloof, untouchable appearance that had once provoked him, ice covering fire. That the fire was there he knew very well, but he also knew that she resented his power to ignite it. He moved towards her.

'Francesca . . .'

She looked up with a blank expression, fearing another hurtful accusation.

'Hadn't you better be off to the casino?' she asked coldly. 'I suppose you won't be back until the small hours?'

His face hardened. Whatever impulse had moved him died away.

'I shall not be home at all,' he told her. 'Perhaps I will be back tomorrow evening, perhaps not. I will ring Luigi when I am sure of my movements.'

144

His eyes met hers, he was smiling cynically. Distinguished in his evening clothes—a must at the casino—perfectly groomed, his smooth black head held high, he looked like a prince of the blood, and as remote.

'*Ciao*,' he said briefly, and was gone.

Francesca felt a gathering constriction round her heart. So there was another woman, and he was reverting to all his former habits. He had never been away all night before. She had known he was there, in the room next to hers, even if he did not come to her. She looked at the well appointed table, set with silver and Venetian glass, the roses in the ornate centrepiece, which she had picked and arranged herself, her one chore. The windows of this small *sala da pranzo* were open to the balcony and the night, the velvet Italian sky above the whispering sea. She could find no fault with her home, except that it was not a home. At last she was beginning to understand her own heart, and she knew that her husband's image filled it. He was infinitely superior to Desmond Watson in every way, apart from his greater physical attractions, and she should have realised it from the start. Instead, she had always sought to withstand him, refusing to open her heart to him, submitting, but never surrendering, her pride demanding that he should not have the triumph of knowing he had won her love.

She would have given anything to be able to recall the terrible words that she had flung at him on their marriage night. He had said he would never forgive them and he was determined to deny her any chance to make amends. Somewhere, some time, she had read that there were three things which could never be taken back—the spent arrow, the spoken word and the lost opportunity. The last two had for her an all too bitter truth.

Luigi came in to tell her that the coffee percolator had been placed in the *salotto*.

'*Grazie*,' she murmured mechanically, resisting an impulse to declare that she did not want any coffee. There would be only one cup—Luigi was always kept apprised of his master's movements. She rose from the table to go into the empty *salotto*. Her dignity demanded that she must keep up appearances before the staff, never betray that all was not as it should be, and not only her dignity but Angelo's.

The languorous heat of summer gave place to a cooler autumn, the olives ripened and the task of gathering them began. Nets were spread under the trees and the fruit was shaken down on to them, the steplike terraces on which the trees were planted obviating the use of ladders, which would have been impracticable on the steep slopes. Old women, their brown faces wrinkled and seamed by time and hard living, picked over the fallen fruit to extricate leaves and other foreign matter.

Bellavista, contrary to expectations, yielded a good crop. On one of her occasional visits to the Castello, Francesca looked down on the scene of activity about her old home. An agent looked after the estate and had been put in as tenant. His brood of thin, brown-skinned, black-eyed children ran laughing up and down the terraces. Francesca watched them wistfully, wishing they were hers. She disliked visiting the Marchese, resenting his swift glance at her waistline, the unspoken question in his eyes. So far she had failed in the main purpose of his son's marriage.

As time passed, she and Angelo drifted further and further apart. Between the olive harvest and his evening amusements she often did not see him for days together, and more and more frequently he did not return at night. There was always an excuse, for Luigi's benefit—he had to go away on business, some crisis demanded that he stayed in Oneglia—but they seemed to her to be flimsy. Tormented by jealousy, she would toss on her lonely bed, longing for his presence, but when he did come she was cold and unresponsive, convinced he only approached her from a sense of duty. She grew pale and languid, and Angelo wanted her to see a doctor.

'I'm all right,' she told him listlessly. 'The heat of last summer drained me. I'll be better now it's cooler.'

She refused steadfastly to seek medical aid. It was not her body that was ailing, but her mind.

Stella had been ill and it was discovered that she would have to have an operation. The doctor who was attending her recommended an English surgeon, a specialist in her particular trouble. Since she was still a British subject and entitled to state aid, while Henry had an insular prejudice against Italian hospitals, it was decided she should be flown to London. She wanted Francesca to go with her. Henry was reluctant to jeopardise his job by a possibly long absence, and was hopeful that his daughter would be able to accompany her mother in his stead.

Francesca welcomed the chance of a break in a routine that was becoming almost insupportable, but she was doubtful if Angelo would let her go. To her surprise he approved wholeheartedly.

'A change would do you good,' he told her. 'Put some colour back into those pale cheeks, though England at this time of year will be shrouded in fog.'

'It's not always so,' she said, recalling mild, still days, lit by a pale sun.

Perversely his concurrence displeased her; it roused

her worst suspicions. She was sure that he wanted her away so that he could pursue his dissolute pleasures unhampered by her presence, for so long as she was at the villa he had to preserve some appearance of fidelity.

'You need a holiday,' Angelo insisted.

'Away from you?' she suggested.

He turned away, shrugging his shoulders. 'Possibly a short separation might be beneficial to us both.'

'Perhaps you'll take one too?' She was watching him closely. 'There'll be winter sports in the Dolomites very soon.'

She knew he had been a keen skier, and the après-ski presented many diversions, some of them amorous.

'Attractive as the idea is, I have too much to do. Father is becoming less and less active. I have a great deal to see to.'

Although the Vittorinis were the principal partners in the olive oil firm, Francesca always found it difficult to associate Angelo with business management. He looked too ornamental to be a tycoon.

As if sensing her thought, he smiled and said: 'I do work for my living, you know.'

'It wasn't always so, was it?'

'I was fortunate, *mio padre* allowed me to have my fun, but there comes a time when one must put away childish things.'

'Your recreations were hardly that.'

'Exactly that. They were rather futile. Ah me, responsibility is ageing. A few more years and I will be getting a bald head and a paunch.'

She glanced at his flat stomach and thick hair.

'I see no danger of that for a long while yet.'

'Do you not? But Maria said...' He broke off as her eyes flashed.

'So you're still seeing that woman?'

'I cannot avoid her,' he returned mildly. 'Didn't you know she is a director in the oil company?'

Francesca was astonished. 'A woman in business? In Italy?'

'Yes, women are infiltrating everywhere. Her father, you see, is a big shareholder, and having no son, he has deputed Maria to represent him.'

This information was singularly unpalatable to Francesca. Her husband was in contact, possibly daily contact, with her enemy. Was it she whom Angelo was with, on the nights he stayed in Oneglia?

'Surely you don't approve of that,' she said acidly. 'You believe a woman's place is in the home.'

'Times change, and Maria is rather exceptional. Her mother is an incurable invalid and her father depends upon her a great deal. Of course he wants her to marry, but she does not seem to be that way inclined.' (No, because she can't get you, Francesca thought.) 'She may lack beauty, but she has a very good brain,' Angelo spoke with reluctant admiration, adding as an afterthought, 'And a very nice figure.'

'What a pity you didn't marry her,' Francesca cried, stung by this appreciation of her rival. 'You have so much in common.'

To her chagrin, this time he did not contradict her, instead he said calmly:

'One of the might-have-beens, but that is always a most unprofitable line of conjecture.'

So he had come to regret his rejection of Maria Donizetti, and that was a most uncomfortable thought for Francesca to carry away with her to England.

Francesca had expected that Angelo would go with her to the airport, but at the last moment some crisis developed in the firm, and it was Henry who accompanied his wife to Genoa in a hired car. Thinking that he would be taking them to catch their flight, she had not even said goodbye to her husband, nor did she see him on the morning of her departure. He had risen very early before she was awake and gone to Imperia. She had a hazy impression that he had bent over her in the darkness before dawn, and kissed her forehead, of his voice murmuring, '*Addio, amore mia,*' on a tender note, but in view of their present relationship, she surmised that she had dreamed it. He had not called her *amore mia* for a very long time.

The fact that she had not said goodbye to him fretted her out of all proportion to its triviality. It seemed to her a fatal omission, though she could not think why, but she had been married to him for nearly six months, and he had never left her without a polite salutation, even though it was only an empty formula.

'I'll be ringing up every day,' Henry told them as they waited in the airport lounge for their flight to be called. 'Vittorini says I may use the firm's telephone. Your husband, Fran, has been more than generous to us all.' He looked at her, his eyes twinkling. 'Luckily for us, he's very much in love with you.'

Francesca smiled but made no rejoinder to this misapprehension. Angelo had been generous with material benefits, he was naturally open-handed, but as for being in love, his heart, his spirit, the essential man were as distant from her as the stars. He had only come close to her physically, and how unsatisfying that was, when she longed for his confidence, his companionship. They were not even friends, in fact at times he seemed like an enemy.

A raucous voice over the tannoy cut short her musings, and Henry kissed his wife.

'Time to go, darling. My thoughts will be with you

day and night.'

Stella, very wan and pale, clung to her daughter's arm, as she assisted her into the conveyance that was to take them over the tarmac to the waiting plane, while Henry waved to them from the barrier.

The jet ran past the assembled shipping in Genoa's fine harbour, and soared up into the clear morning sky. Francesca had a sudden premonition that she would never see Italy again.

Francesca was accommodated in a quiet hotel in Bloomsbury while her mother was in hospital. The surgeon would not perform the operation until Stella was thoroughly rested from her journey, and the delay was trying for all concerned. Henry rang, as he promised, every day. The Marchese rang her up more than once, enquiring about her health and Stella's, but Angelo did not ring at all.

Eventually the day of Stella's ordeal came, a period of acute anxiety. She came through satisfactorily, but it was several days before Francesca was allowed to see her. As soon as she was well enough she was to be transferred to a private nursing home, where a room had been engaged for her at the Vittorinis' expense, as it would be some time before she was fit to travel to Italy.

Except for her visits to the hospital, time passed slowly for Francesca. London seemed strange and unfriendly after her long sojourn in the warmth and conviviality of Italy. She looked up one or two old friends from her college days, girls who were living in flatlets and were were deeply involved in amorous adventures. She found them irritating, their so-called modern outlook trivial and vulgar. She did not go again. She read a good deal and wrote frequently to her father describing her mother's progress. She also wrote to Stacey, and a brief letter to Angelo. This last was not easy, there was so much she wanted to say, but dared not put into words. At the finish it was no more than a brief recital of her small doings, but she hoped that he would answer it.

December came in and the weather turned dull and blustery, though Henry told them it was warm and sunny in Liguria. Stacey informed her that Angelo had taken her out upon several occasions to console her for her mother's and sister's absence. Kind of him, Francesca thought, but then he was kind and thoughtful to everyone except herself. No doubt he was further alienating her from Stacey.

Nevertheless she waited eagerly for a letter from him, for though he had not telephoned, and he could not find her activities very interesting, she was sure he would be too courteous to let her own epistle go unanswered.

One evening, desperate with yearning to hear his voice, she rang the villa. Luigi answered it, saying his master was out. She could hardly expect that he would dine alone in an empty house, but nevertheless she felt sick with disappointment. When next he rang, she asked her father-in-law how her husband was faring. The Marchese said he was well and very busy; there was a guarded note in his voice which scared her.

Stella's nursing home was at Hampstead, and Francesca travelled there by tube, but found the underground made her feel unwell. She changed to a bus, but it was no better. Finally she went by taxi. After all, Angelo had provided her with plenty of money, and there was no real need for economy, but she continued to feel nausea. She supposed the travelling and change of climate had affected her.

At last she received a letter from Angelo. She opened it with trembling fingers, thinking how seldom she had seen his forcible black script. It began abruptly:

Francesca,

Once not so long ago you asked me to let you go, and I refused, since a separation did not seem to me to be the solution of our problems. Since then I have given much thought to that request, and have decided that your demand was not unreasonable, for it is only too obvious to me that you are unhappy, and unlikely to be anything else while you are with me. I ought never to have married you, but I hoped—however, never mind that now. I am not as you persist in thinking a lustful monster, nor am I insensitive to your aversion, and the present situation is painful to me too. I propose therefore to end it. Though in this country divorce is not yet recognised, in certain circumstances it is possible to obtain a dissolution. Since we have no children and you are not of my faith it may not be too difficult. While negotiations are pending, please do not attempt to contact me, which would jeopardise their success. Until you wed again, as you are sure to do if I can obtain your freedom, I will continue to pay your allowance into your bank in London. I hope that my decision will lead you to the felicity which was so impossible as my wife. Angelo Vittorini.

P.S. I would ask that you will revert to your own name.

Francesca read and re-read the searing lines, sensing what they did not say, the bitterness of wounded vanity and hurt pride. Knowing that she did not love him, he had expected during their short engagement to be able to bring her to his feet. Instead she had sought to leave him for another man. Yet the fault was not wholly hers; many times in the past few months she would have tried gladly to heal the breach, if he had shown any warmth of feeling, but he had shut himself away from her. All she had known of him was his body; his mind was a closed book to her.

With feminine logic, she was certain that what lay behind this desire for freedom was another woman, probably Maria Donizetti, who had been the evil genius of her married life. Maria's cruel words came back to her—'She is insipid, you will be satiated with her within a week.' It had been rather longer than that, but it no longer amused Angelo to overcome her reluctance, a reluctance which she had long ceased to feel. When last Angelo had spoken of Maria it had been with regret for a might-have-been. She might be plain, but she was clever and she had bided her time. She must have convinced him that she possessed a fire and passion to match his own.

Casting back in her mind, Francesca realised that she had never once given Angelo an affectionate demonstration. Since their marriage night she had been checked by his withdrawal, and it was only now, when she had lost him, that she knew how deeply she loved him.

Folding the letter, she put it back in its envelope, while a cold desolation crept over her. Subconsciously she had been counting the days until she could return to Italy, the sun, the warmth and Angelo. Rain beat against the window from out of a grey sky and the room felt chilly. England was exile to her now.

She stood up, feeling sudden nausea, and the room seemed to swim before her eyes. Staggering towards the bell, she fell down in a faint.

CHAPTER EIGHT

'WELL, Mrs Vittorini,' the doctor said, 'there's nothing to worry about, in fact you are to be congratulated. I can't be certain without making a test, but hasn't it occurred to you that you might be pregnant?'

Francesca wondered why it had not, for there had been signs which she should have recognised, but she had attributed them to the change of climate and the various anxieties to which she had been subject recently. Only yesterday, when she had fainted, had she suspected, and she had come this morning to have her suspicion confirmed.

'Well, actually, what with the air trip, which sometimes upsets me, and one thing and another, I hadn't thought of it,' she admitted.

The irony of the situation struck her, and she nearly laughed. Just when Angelo had decided to free her, she had discovered she was to bear his child!

'Your husband is with you?' the doctor asked.

Francesca shook her head. 'He couldn't leave Italy,' and she proceeded to explain about her mother.

The doctor heard her out with a perplexed frown. The position seemed a little odd to him. Two husbands had allowed their wives to come alone to England, one to face a critical operation, and the other was showing obvious signs of strain, more than anxiety about her mother warranted, especially since her mother was now out of danger. She was a lovely-looking girl, he thought, and it would be a shame if extra-marital complications were at the root of her trouble, for she would need all the help and sustenance she could obtain in the days to come.

'You will be returning soon?' he suggested.

'I ... I suppose so.'

'You should do so as soon as possible. You need rest and care, Mrs Vittorini, you don't look very robust. You have your own doctor in Italy, of course, and you would do well to consult him as soon as you get back. Perhaps your husband is coming to fetch you? If so, I'd like a word with him.'

'He won't be able to get away,' Francesca said quickly. She looked uneasily at the consultant, not liking the way in which he was studying her. 'There isn't anything wrong, is there?'

He hastened to reassure her. All would be well so long as she was sensible and took good care of herself. She must be careful not to over-exert herself. He reiterated that she should return to her home as soon as possible.

He watched her walk out of his consulting room with a slight frown, his eyes on her narrow hips.

Francesca left the surgery on a wave of exultation. There could be no question of a dissolution now. When she told Angelo he would be as delighted as she was, and with this new bond between them he must surely forgive her.

She wanted to ring him up there and then, and her nerves quivered in anticipation of hearing his voice, thinking how his cold greeting would change to warmth when she made known to him the reason for her call. Stella was nearly fit to travel, and he might offer to come and fetch them. At the prospect of seeing him again so soon, her spirits soared.

At that time of day Angelo would probably be at his office, but Francesca remembered he was guarded by a dragon of a secretary who would not relay her call unless she said who she was. A shadow touched her joy, like that cast on the sun by the moon, before a total eclipse. He might, when she gave her name, refuse to speak to her. He had said that she must not contact him.

It was unlikely that she could catch him at the villa; he so often went out and might not return there at all. It seemed, upon reflection, that her best course was to write to him. She found her missive exceedingly difficult to compose, after what he had written to her. She read his letter again, and the cruel sentences stabbed her afresh. But the child would make all the difference. Its coming must heal the breach between them.

Yet when it came to the point, she was curiously shy about admitting her coming motherhood on paper. She wanted to be able to see his face and test his reaction. Finally she merely stated that she had something very important to tell him, and would he please ring her up at her hotel. She would at least hear his voice.

The next day she went to see her mother. Angelo would not get her letter for several days, so there was no point in sitting by the phone waiting for his call, not for some time yet.

Stella was up and dressed and staring disconsolately out at the grey sky outside which held a hint of snow to come. She was longing to go home, for she hated the English winter, which she had not had to endure for many years. Every day she had been asking how much longer must she wait.

As she came in, Francesca noticed how well she was looking; there could be no reason for longer delay in implementing both their wishes. She would arrange for their flight home and when Angelo contacted her she would be able to tell him when to expect them and ask him about arranging to meet them at Genoa.

Stella turned from the window and her face flashed into animation. She had her own bed-sitting-room in the expensive home where she had been installed, so their privacy was not interrupted.

'Lovely news, darling,' she exclaimed eagerly, as Francesca kissed her. 'I'm to go home the day after tomorrow! Henry has given me the name and address of a family who are going out to Genoa and with whom I can travel. I'm to meet them at the airport, and my flight has been booked. Oh, how thankful I shall be to see the last of this place!'

This news took Francesca aback. Her father had accepted that she would not be returning herself, but who had told him? Angelo, presumably, but what reason could he have given for her continued stay in London?

Stella proceeded to enlighten her. Recalling herself from her own affairs, she surveyed her daughter with a puzzled frown.

'Henry says you aren't coming back, and Angelo has sent your personal belongings to our flat. He's giving up the villa. What on earth has happened, Fran?'

Shattered by this sudden information that she had lost her home, and unwilling to tell her mother the truth, Francesca murmured vaguely the first explanation that occurred to her.

'Angelo wants to make ... er ... other arrangements. Live nearer to his work.'

'But he was only seven kilometres from Oneglia where you were, and it was such a pretty house,' Stella said regretfully.

Francesca's lips trembled as she recalled the day when she and Angelo had first viewed their prospective home, and he had asked her if she could be happy there. That she had not been so was her own fault, but

158

she had hoped to remedy that; now the chance had gone for ever.

Angelo had acted with extreme promptitude, anxious to obliterate all memory of her from his life. She remembered with a prick of jealousy that Maria Donizetti was working at Oneglia. Was it possible that she was setting up a joint household with Angelo at Imperia? Once, how long ago it seemed, she had declared that she had lived with Angelo, and Francesca had never wholly believed his denial. But since both were prominent in the firm, they could hardly do that now; both had appearances to observe, though there was no reason why Angelo should not seek solace in Maria's company, and she probably had a flat near her work.

Stella's thoughts were already turning back to her own affairs. Since Francesca had been taken over by her grandmother, she had shown very little interest in her elder daughter's concerns, and her absorption in her own health and wellbeing had made her entirely self-centred.

'I suppose everything's all right between you?' she asked vaguely.

Francisca had an impulse to confide in her. Stella was after all her mother, the person to whom she should tell her difficulties, who ought to give her sympathy, and perhaps advice. She looked wistfully at Stella's still pretty, empty face, while she hesitated. Her mother was turning over Henry's letter and making a note of a telephone number on a piece of paper.

'Perhaps you'd give these people a ring?' she asked. 'I believe they've got my ticket. Just check that everything is in order. I'd hate there to be a hitch. I feel I can't bear this place any longer,'

She had not even waited for an answer to her question.

'Yes, certainly,' Francesca promised, taking the slip of paper. There was no help to be had from Stella; she was completely uninterested. Francesca had a sudden longing for her grandmother. The old lady would have had a solution for any dilemma, and she would have been like a lioness in her granddaughter's defence.

The news that Angelo had given up the villa had shaken her badly, it seemed so irrevocable. If she returned, where was she going to live? Where was Angelo living—officially? Perhaps he would insist that she went to the Castello to await her child's coming. She remembered that the Marchese had said that Angelo's *bambini* ought to be raised there. The idea was unpleasant, she had never liked the Vittorinis' ancestral home; it was too vast, too permeated with the atmosphere of the past, and a murky past at that. Her first impression of it had been that it would be a prison for Angelo's bride, while he pursued his diversions elsewhere. That had been before she met him. She could not bear to live under the stern eyes of the Marchese, who saw in her only a means to an end. She had never thought he liked her very much as a person.

She said goodbye to her mother without mentioning either the baby or her estrangement from her husband, with a reiterated promise to ring up her prospective travelling companions.

Stella departed before Francesca had received an answer from Angelo, and she went with her mother to see her off.

'I suppose you'll be coming back soon yourself?' Stella asked, without much interest. 'When Angelo has found a new house? Or does he expect you to live at that gloomy Castello? I suppose running two establishments was a bit expensive, even for the Vittorinis, but I should advise you to put your foot down about that. The castle may be very fine, but it gave me the creeps.'

'It is a little over-awing,' Francesca agreed non-committally. 'I certainly would prefer to live somewhere else.'

Stella's fellow travellers came up to claim her, and nothing more was said about Francesca's return.

She watched the plane take off with wistful eyes, wishing she too was going home, then remembered that she had no home to which to go. But perhaps it was not too late. Angelo might not have given up the lease of the house, but had merely moved out of it.

Two days later her letter to Angelo was returned to her, enclosed in a typewritten envelope. It had not been opened. She was informed curtly in the accompanying note that under the circumstances Signor Vittorini wished to receive no personal correspondence from her. Any queries that she wanted to make should be sent to his solicitors, the name and address of the firm being quoted. The letter was also typed and signed by Angelo's secretary. She felt she had been given a blow in the face.

By the same mail came a smudged and tear-stained letter from Stacey.

'Angelo says you won't come back, ever. Fran, please, please do. It isn't like it used to be, and Angelo is so sad. He's left your lovely house, he says you didn't like it, but you did. Please, please, come back and tell him so. Oh, Fran, we're all so miserable without you. You must come home.'

The piteous note wrung Francesca's heart, echoing as it did her own longings. Happiness seemed to be retreating beyond recall. As he had done for so many weeks, Angelo had shut himself away from her, refusing to listen to any plea she made. She smiled a little wryly. This time he had deliberately cut himself off from what he most desired to hear. She could tell the Marchese, or her own people, and ask them to inform him, but that she would not do. It was her right and privilege to tell him herself, and since he had made himself inaccessible, he should remain in ignorance.

She began to search for a small flat.

To Stacey she sent a magnificent Christmas present with an evasive reply to her letter. She also sents gifts and good wishes to her parents. Their acknowledgments were stiff and formal, indicating that they all considered her at fault. Possibly Angelo had told them that she refused to return, which was unfair, but he would have to say something. Since they were so beholden to him they would naturally take his part.

Christmas with its emphasis on the birth of the Holy Child was unbearably poignant.

'For unto us a Child is born.'

To her and Angelo a child was to be given, but she began to wonder if he would really appreciate it; he would do so only if it were a boy. She was quite confident that it would be, and as such, it would be heir to the Vittorini name and possessions. Rather a burden for the poor mite, she thought a little sadly, especially if it inherited her own sense of responsibility, which the young Angelo had apparently lacked.

She found a small furnished flat and moved into it. After which she fell into a curious state of lethargy. She was waiting, though she was not quite sure for what. Possibly Angelo's next move, which might be the information that a dissolution could be obtained, or a counter-proposal if it were impossible.

She had no compunction about using his money, though she would not have touched it under other circumstances. It amused her to think that he was unwittingly providing for his own child. It also seemed amusing that he was pulling strings in the endeavour to free himself from her, when if he knew the true situation he would be falling over himself to get her back again.

Alone in her little flat, her days passed tranquilly, but often in the night she would awake with the tears streaming down her face and an aching void in her heart. Angelo—her child's father, how she longed for him! At such moments she resolved to go back to Italy and confront him with his fatherhood, but when the morning light came, she again procrastinated, assailed by doubts and fears which were exaggerated by her condition. The forbidding grandeur of the Castello haunted her. She could not, would not, allow her child to be born there. She became convinced that the Marchese and Angelo would do their best to take her son away from her, remembering how exclusive Angelo had been over Stacey. It was only too possible that, hating her as he appeared to do, her husband would set himself to win the boy's affections away from her, which with his gaiety and charm he could quite easily do. Instead of being a bond, the child might prove to be another bone of contention. She needed the baby badly herself, someone to love her and upon whom to bestow her love.

Again, it would not be a good life for a child to be torn between estranged parents, in fact it might be better for him if he never knew his father.

So she argued with herself, and fretted, unable to decide which course to pursue, or to sort out her tangled emotions. She longed for Angelo, and at the same time was deeply incensed against him for his treatment of her. She passionately desired that he should know about the child, and at the same time dreaded that he might try to take it from her.

Always the Castello loomed large in her imagination. She could not make up her mind if she regarded it as a prison or a sanctuary, the former because she might find herself practically incarcerated in it, the latter because it was where Angelo appeared to be living.

She did not again visit the doctor, who had told her to go home, but attended a nearby maternity clinic, where everybody was much too busy to be interested in her marital problems. There was no doubt now but that she was *enceinte* and she was advised that as it was her first, she would probably have to go into hospital. This suited her, having no one to look after her, and to obviate awkward questions she declared herself a widow, and gave her father as her next of kin.

Having acquired a liking for Italian food, Francesca often went to lunch at a small restaurant in Soho run by Italians. It was not only the food that attracted her, the proprietor and his waiters were Italians and often spoke to each other in their mother tongue. That and the atmosphere of the place were reminiscent of Italy, and she was nostalgic for Liguria.

One day she saw a familiar figure come in and seat herself at the next table. There was no mistaking the heavy features, and the elegant shape dressed discreetly in a well cut black suit and wearing black furs. Maria Donizetti raised her eyes from the menu card and encountered Francesca's gaze, and instantly recognised her. Rather to Francesca's surprise, she stood up and came across to her.

'*Ciao, signora,*' she said, 'this is an unexpected meeting.' Her eyes ran over the other girl inquisitively. Francesca was wearing a dark cloth coat trimmed lav-

164

ishly with grey fur, which concealed the as yet slight thickening of her waist, long suede boots and a small grey fur cap, from under which her hair curled softly about her face. Its pure oval was pale, her unusual eyes, dark and mysterious, the pupils dilated, and her smile was faintly secretive. She looked like a young witch poring over a mystic potion, instead of the risotto on her plate.

Maria sighed enviously. She could see what had enchanted Angelo about this girl, and she blamed her entirely for the rift between them, a rift she had sought by every subtle means in her power to widen. Of its real cause she was ignorant, but she surmised from unguarded remarks that Angelo had dropped that the girl was frigid and antipathetic to the Italian mode of life. Yet, if he could see her now, with the delicate bloom that seemed to emanate from her soft skin, the reason for which she did not suspect, he would surely be enchained afresh, but Maria hoped very much that he would never see his wife again.

'Won't you join me?' Francesca asked, for although she had no reason to like Maria, she was a link with her life in Liguria, for which she was hankering, and she was close to Angelo. At risk of being wounded, she hoped she would mention his name. Maria must know what he was doing, might be led on to talk about him, tell her where he was living. Her parents' scanty letters never mentioned him and she was too proud to ask for news herself.

Maria accepted her invitation. Both had come to the restaurant for the same reason—it served the best Italian food in London.

'I am over here to put through a deal,' Maria explained her presence. 'You know I am a business woman nowadays. I enjoy working, though I have been criticised for taking a job when I do not need one.'

'If you're blessed with brains, it's a pity not to find a use for them,' Francesca suggested, recalling that Angelo had admitted this woman's intelligence.

'Very nicely put. Unfortunately the people who need work are so often useless morons,' Maria said briskly. She looked at the girl opposite to her speculatively. 'Are you also working?'

'Not at the moment, but I may get a job later on,' Francesca told her evasively, and saw a faint scorn in Maria's eyes. She knows I must be living on Angelo, Francesca thought, and despises me for it. The knowledge did not hurt, for there was a reason for her dependence that Maria did not know.

Throughout the meal they talked upon various impersonal subjects. Maria liked London, but thought its climate was appalling. To Francesca's disappointment, she said little about Imperia and did not mention the Vittorinis. But when they had reached the coffee stage, Maria leaned back in her chair, and said coolly:

'So you have left him?'

Francesca stiffened, unprepared for such bluntness.

'It isn't really your business,' she said quietly, 'or do you consider it is?'

Maria smiled a little grimly.

'Under certain circumstances, it might be,' she stated. 'You're a fool, you know, to let him go. *Dio mio!*' She relapsed into her own language. 'How could you do it? Angelo is a king among men, he has everything, and he wanted to give you everything, and yet you threw him away.'

Francesca winced. Maria's words held a grain of truth. She had only learned to appreciate her husband when it was too late, but she was not going to be brow-

166

beaten by a woman who she suspected was hoping to benefit from the situation.

'You don't know all the circumstances,' she pointed out. 'I suppose Angelo has given you his point of view, but I have one too.'

'Obviously, and it seems to be diametrically opposed to his,' Maria remarked drily. 'But then I could see from the very start that you were not the right woman for him—a chilly little Northern icicle. I gather you dared to disapprove of his morals?'

'He told you that?'

'He said once that you had difficulty in distinguishing between him and the character he assumed for a fancy dress dance.'

'He rather fancied himself in the diabolical role,' Francesca said brightly, though inwardly she was stabbed. Angelo could never forgive nor forget her foolish words. 'By the way, how is he?' she asked, and waited breathlessly for Maria's reply.

'Not regretting you, my girl,' Maria told her tartly. 'He has been behaving like a boy out of school since you went away. He has entered for the Monte Carlo Rally, and he is out most nights on the town, while as for company——' She gave Francesca a malicious glance. 'Ever heard of Vera Verachi?'

As it happened Francesca had. Vera Verachi was a beautiful, amoral socialite, whose doings were pictured in all the glossy magazines. She would be a rival far more formidable than Maria.

'You don't mean——?' she asked doubtfully.

'That she has annexed him? They have been seen about together, so she probably has. She presents a challenge, you see, and that Angelo never could resist. She has so many men courting her favours.' A tinge of bitterness crept into Maria's voice. She had had some bad moments over Vera herself.

Francesca crumbled the remains of her roll, while her heart sank.

'Do you think he'll be able to get this dissolution?' she asked faintly.

'Eventually he may, but it will take a long time. He will keep on pressing for it, of course, since it is essential that he should have a son.'

Francesca became engrossed in her breadcrumbs.

'Does he plan to marry this Vera person?' she asked, trying to sound indifferent.

'Oh no, he would never marry her.' Maria sounded shocked at the notion, and Francesca's heart lightened. 'She is much too notorious.'

An echo from the past, a voice murmuring, 'A man likes to be sure his children are his own.' One of her own assets had been her integrity, but that had got her nowhere.

Maria went on quickly, as if to reassure herself, 'He has to marry again because he is the last of his family. It is inconceivable that the line should be allowed to die out. Angelo must have a son. The Veras of this world avoid having children. So, it seems, did you.' Her deep-set eyes flicked over Francesca speculatively —perhaps that had been the cause of the break-up.

Francesca said nothing. Angelo had been too impatient. If only he had waited a while, she would not now be facing her present dilemma.

'With that in mind, he will select his next bride with more regard for her suitability,' Maria concluded.

Francesca flashed a quizzical look at her.

'Yourself, for example?' she queried.

'Why not? I could make him a good wife. It was suggested, you know, before you came on the scene with Bellavista up your sleeve. He does not love me, but I can get along without that.'

In spite of this assertion her eyes were bleak, and Francesca felt a twinge of pity for her. She herself had come to know the pain of unrequited love. She said sadly:

'I don't think there can be much happiness in a marriage when only one of the partners loves.'

Maria glanced at her shrewdly. 'Was that your experience?'

'Oh, leave me out of it, I'm a back number now.'

'At least you have the sense to realise it,' Maria observed. 'He was crazy about you at the beginning.' Francesca blinked—surely that could not be true? 'But nothing would induce him to take you back again.'

Francesca lowered her lashes to conceal the triumphant gleam in her eyes. Maria was wrong there.

'I shouldn't be too sure about that,' she warned her opponent.

Maria looked perturbed. 'I understood the separation was permanent.'

She stared at Francesca so penetratingly that the latter feared she had guessed her secret.

'That depends,' she said carefully. 'He may not be able to obtain this dissolution, and it may take a long time if he does.'

'But couldn't you divorce him?' Maria asked eagerly. 'I do not know how you stand with regard to that, but if you regain your British nationality, you can plead desertion after two years.'

'It would not be valid in Italy, and two years is a long time,' Francesca pointed out.

Maria shrugged her shoulders. 'Time soon goes, and surely you will want to make ... other arrangements?'

Apparently she suspected the existence of another attachment. No doubt Angelo had hinted as much; he had told her in his letter that he was sure she would marry again.

Francesca said nothing, but something in her expression alarmed Maria. She said anxiously:

'You would not, of course, dream of returning to Italy? It would give Angelo's application more chance of success if you stayed out of the country.'

'I don't think I can do that. My family are still in Italy, and I should like to visit them. They are all I have now.'

'But they live in Imperia,' Maria protested, 'and if you go there, the odds are you might run into Angelo, and that would be fatal.'

Her small eyes narrowed suspiciously, and Francesca realised that the woman opposite to her still feared her influence over Angelo and that if he met her he would want her back again. It was a heartening idea, but she was sure it was groundless, she herself was of no value to him, but what she carried might be.

Maria's hopeless love deserved some compassion, but she had also shown herself to be an unscrupulous enemy. Francesca was fairly certain that she had done her best to fan Angelo's resentment against herself. Seeing him daily she would have many opportunities of catching him in a despondent or confidential mood and she would not miss any chance to denigrate the absent wife. Maria wanted her man, and since Francesca had abdicated, so to speak, she already saw herself as the next occupant of the throne.

'I will be very careful,' Francesca promised, 'but you can't expect me to accept separation from my family indefinitely.'

Maria said eagerly: 'If you let me know when you

are coming, I will make sure Angelo keeps out of your way.'

'Thank you so much, that would be a relief,' Francesca told her with forced sweetness, disguising how Maria's assumption of authority over her husband was needling her.

'So long as you realise how important it is that you should not meet Angelo, even accidentally,' Maria urged.

Francesca reflected with a pang that if there was a chance encounter, Angelo would probably cut her—until he knew. The thing Maria feared was a reconciliation, and that was why she wanted to keep Francesca away from Liguria, or if she must come, be able to keep a watch upon her movements. She little knew that if Francesca did return, it would be to go straight to her husband. Francesca fastened her coat and reached for her gloves and bag, signalling to the waiter to bring her bill.

'I'm afraid I must go now,' she said politely. 'It has been so nice meeting you, Signorina Donizetti, and thank you for your advice.' She hesitated, recalling all Maria had told her. 'Is she really very beautiful?' she blurted out.

'Who?' Maria looked surprised.

'This Vera Verachi.'

The waiter's approach diverted Maria's attention.

'Let this be on me,' she said, reaching for her purse.

Francesca forestalled her. 'On the contrary, let me treat you,' she said, passing the waiter several notes. 'You are a guest in my country, and you have been most informative.'

Maria did not argue and expressed her thanks a little curtly. Francesca guessed that she did not like

171

being beholden to her, and that was why she had done it.

As they reached the street, Maria said:

'Vera Verachi is an exceptionally lovely woman, but she is also extremely fickle, so I do not consider she is a great menace.' She sighed regretfully as she often did when forced to contemplate her own lack of beauty. She went on confidently:

'But even if she does not tire of him or he of her, he will have to give her up.' She looked at Francesca significantly. 'Neither you, nor Vera, nor any woman, though she was as beautiful as Venus and as beguiling, can compete with Angelo's need for a son.'

With which parting shot she bade a formal farewell and hurried away across the road. Francesca stood where she was, watching Maria's elegant figure dive through the traffic, a little smile edging her lips. Poor Maria, she little knew what she was up against.

Then she too sighed as she walked away. Her talk with Maria had brought Angelo vividly back into her mind—his beautiful enigmatical face, his lean bronzed body, the tones of his voice, so often mocking, occasionally, but very rarely, tender. It hurt her to know that he was expending all his charm upon this unknown lovely, seeking perhaps to soothe the vanity which she had wounded. One at least of the accusations she had thrown at him was true, he would never really love a woman, he had too great a contempt for women, and she doubted if he could experience that emotion as she understood it. He had never, even when he was most ardent, told her that he loved her. His feeling for her had been a passing infatuation, quickly satisfied. Rejoicing in his freedom, he had gone back to his gay bachelor life and Vera was only another 'episode'. But in spite of all his faults, his weaknesses, nothing could kill her own love for him. As Maria had said, he had everything, except perhaps fidelity.

Maria had insisted that he could not be free for long, and whatever his sentiments towards women, Francesca knew that he would adore his son.

Upon returning to her hotel, Francesca resolved to end the present situation. It was hardly fair to Maria to let it continue. Besides, she too had some rights, for she was still Angelo's wife, and the time had come to assert them. As she was the prospective mother of his son, he must accord her some consideration. The child was all-important, and she was grateful to Maria for dissipating her hesitation. She would get in touch with her husband that very night and put an end to Vera's wiles and Maria's subtle planning.

She waited until the hour when she knew Angelo usually dined and put a call through to the Castello.

It took some time to get her connection, and when the telephone was eventually answered, she recognised the voice as Luigi's. So Angelo was actually living with his father. Hoping the man would not recognise hers, she asked for the Marchese.

'It is a matter of great importance,' she told Luigi in her best Italian, 'but it is very private.'

Here she received a check. Antonio Vittorini had gone away for a few days' hunting in the mountains. With fast beating heart, she asked for Signor Angelo.

Luigi was full of apologies—he too was absent, a dinner date, but if the matter was very urgent, he could be contacted at the flat of Signora Verachi. If Madame wished, he would give her the number.

Madame declined, and when Luigi asked for her name and a message, she rang off.

Having keyed herself up to make her disclosure,

Francesca felt flattened. Her indignation welled up against Angelo. Though Luigi's information only confirmed what Maria had told her, it brought the situation forcibly home to her. She was lonely and unhappy, while he was amusing himself with one of Europe's most notorious women in between visits to the casino and motor racing. What sort of a father would he be for her son? A gambler and a rake, and suppose after all the child was not a boy? He would have no use for a daughter and be all the more bitter for the disappointment. She thought of all the other possibilities that might occur. She might not go full term, the child could be stillborn or imperfect—frightening hazards for prospective parents and ones for which Angelo would give her little sympathy if they materialised. He would feel that he had taken her back under false pretences.

She recalled the doctor's dubious looks when she had first been apprised of her condition. Had he foreseen that something would go wrong? Pregnant women are often fanciful, and Francesca's imaginings took a morbid turn.

There were still months of waiting to be endured, during which she would lose her figure, and the fastidious Angelo might turn from her in disgust. He would certainly neglect her and if there was going to be a succession of Veras she did not want to have them brought to her notice first hand. She admitted that in the present instance he considered he was at the moment free, which she supposed excused his conduct with Vera, and while she had lived with him, she had had no actual proof that he was unfaithful, but she could not imagine him being patient with the exigencies of pregnancy.

She decided then that she would wait until the child

was born before trying again to contact its father. If it turned out to be a healthy boy as she prayed and hoped, she would return to Italy in triumph, for then she would have a weapon which no other woman could combat. Angelo and the Marchese would be delighted and perhaps a little of their joy would be expended upon the baby's mother.

That in the meantime Angelo might procure his dissolution was a risk she had to take, but she thought it was unlikely since such processes were slow, and surely she would be asked for her acquiescence? She had no idea what the procedure was, but imagined that she would have to sign something or other.

She would guard her secret carefully until the time was ripe, and she would let her coming be a surprise. Her eyes grew soft and her hurt was healed, as she dreamed of the moment when she arrived back in Liguria with her son in her arms. Whatever her own welcome was, she could be sure his would be rapturous.

CHAPTER NINE

ANGELA ANASTASIA VITTORINI was born when midsummer was past, and the July thunderheads were gathering in the sky. She nearly cost her mother her life. She was everything a baby should be. She had black hair and the indeterminate blue eyes of babyhood. Also, as new-born babies sometimes do, she had an almost uncanny likeness to her father; there was no doubt whose child she was.

When the nurse in her bright, professional voice said:

'You have a lovely little daughter, Mrs Vittorini,' and laid the baby beside her, Francesca turned her face to the pillow while the slow tears of extreme weakness oozed from her eyes. There would be no reconciliation since she had failed to give Angelo the longed-for son.

Since the hospital staff believed her to be a widow, they were all sympathy for her solitary state. It was hard luck that her only relations were so far away. Francesca did not know how nearly her father had been summoned, when it was feared she would not survive.

Being young and resilient, she soon began to regain her strength, and after the initial disappointment, was able to lavish all the love within her starved heart upon her little daughter. The Vittorinis would not want her, because she was a girl, but that made her entirely her mother's possession.

As soon as she was well enough, Francesca went back to her flat and immersed herself in baby care. Angela was a placid and contented baby except upon the rare occasions when she was thwarted, when she roared with a fine display of Vittorini rage.

Francesca's love for her was more than normally protective, since she would be rejected by her haughty kinsmen. Deprived of her birthright, she had only her mother upon whom to rely, not only for her material comfort but for love and understanding.

When she had fully recovered, Francesca took stock of her position. She felt that she could no longer live upon Angelo's bounty since she had failed to give him a son. That would have justified his support, but she herself would provide for the disappointing daughter. She knew that Angelo would not shirk his responsibility towards Angela, but she feared that if he learned of her existence he would try to take her from her, and she was determined that she should not be brought up by a stepmother or be secondary to Angelo's offspring by another wife.

Enquiries soon assured her that she would have no difficulty in obtaining a well-paid post, and Angela could be left during the day at a nursery, where, as she grew older, she would have the benefit of the company of other children.

Then after a silence of many months, she wrote again to Angelo. She told him that she did not feel justified in continuing to accept an allowance from him, and she would much prefer to be independent. She was quite capable of supporting herself. She did not think that it was right that he should continue to maintain her, since she was in fact no longer his wife, and she was sure that he would eventually find a more satisfactory mistress for his home. She could have communicated her decision to his solicitors, but her pride found more satisfaction in conveying it to the man himself. To ensure that her letter would be read, she borrowed a typewriter, and on the envelope enscribed, 'Private. Urgent and Important.' He would not realise who it was from until he had opened it, or so she hoped.

As she sealed her cold epistle, she wondered if Maria had already moved in with him, in the hope that their union could soon be legalised, and to circumvent any more Veras. She felt a constriction round her heart as she thought of Maria's triumph. Would he re-open the villa to accommodate her, and would they use the furniture which she and Angelo had chosen together, and share the bedroom that had once been hers?

Later, much later, when she knew that her connection with Angelo had been finally severed, she would confide in her parents, though she dared not take Angela to Italy. Perhaps Stacey would be allowed to come and stay with her, though whether her sister would ever forgive her leaving Angelo was doubtful. But as the girl grew older, her adoration of Angelo must inevitably fade, and she would come to a greater understanding of the complications involved in marriage. She might even need a refuge one day, if the Vittorinis sought to arrange a partnership for her which she did not desire. Francesca smiled faintly. Stacey had a mind and a will of her own, she would not be coerced in matters of the heart.

The weather turned cold and wet as autumn approached. Francesca found herself longing for the Italian sunshine. She waited with some trepidation for Angelo's reply, but it was long in coming. He might not answer her letter himself, would probably turn it over to his solicitors, but at least it had not been returned unopened. Yet she looked hopefully every morning for a sight of his strong black script.

Meanwhile she went forward with her own plans. She had been offered a situation as cook and caterer at a London hospital, which seemed suitable, and she had found a very modern nursery where Angela could be accommodated. The thought of the day-long separation cost her a pang, but she did not mean to make the same mistake her grandmother had done with herself. Angela would learn to be self-reliant and independent right from the start.

Then one drizzly afternoon, while Angela slept, Francesca had an unexpected visitor.

She went to open the door, all unsuspecting, to find herself face to face with her husband. She was wearing trousers and a flowered smock, her hair loose upon her shoulders, for she had been coping with the daily wash a small baby entails. Her face was innocent of make-up and she looked a mere girl.

Angelo was formally dressed in a business suit, and she noticed in one lightning glance that he looked older, and there was a touch of silver at his temples. Lines, they might have been drawn by sorrow or dissipation, reached from his nostrils to his mouth. They had never been visible before.

One glance, and then she was all confusion, the wild rose colour flooding her cheeks. She had never dreamed that he might reply to her letter in person, and she was thrown off balance.

'May I come in?' he asked politely. 'I think you and I have business to discuss.' Then as she neither moved nor spoke, he added. 'Perhaps I should have given you warning. You look as if His Satanic Majesty himself had arrived on your doorstep, but then you always did associate me with him.'

Ignoring this gibe, she made an effort to pull herself together.

'I ... I was so surprised,' she faltered. 'But do come in.'

She led the way into the small sitting-room of the flat, which comprised two rooms, a kitchenette and a bathroom. Since she had taken it furnished, it showed no mark of her personality, beyond a few books and a picture of Italy, which she had bought and placed over the electric stove in the grate. It showed one of the old narrow streets, and might have been Cervo.

She was wondering why Angelo had thought it necessary to call upon her, and a sudden wild hope shot through her. But a glance at his cold, unresponsive face killed it. He had not come to effect a reconciliation, but probably needed her signature to some document. Luckily Angela had just been fed and was unlikely to wake.

Angelo looked round the far from luxurious interior of the room with distaste.

'I should have thought your allowance would have run to something better than this,' he observed.

'It serves,' she said coolly, now completely mistress of herself. 'Sit down, do. Would you like something— tea? Coffee? I'm afraid I can't run to wine. It's expensive over here.'

'No, thank you.'

He sat down on an upholstered chair, looking as out of place in her small domain as a golden pheasant in a hen roost. His eyes swept over her with the familiar slumbrous glance.

'You appear younger than ever,' he remarked, 'but you look frail. You are quite well?'

'Oh, I'm fine. I expect it's only because I've lost my sunburn.'

The flush his coming had evoked had faded to extreme pallor.

'Not surprising in this atrocious climate.' His eyes went to the window, outside which the London smog was gathering, and returned to her again. She had sat down opposite to him, her long legs crossed, trying to appear completely at her ease.

'What's all this nonsense about taking a job?'

'It isn't nonsense. I'm only starting what I should have done before ...' She broke off, biting her lip, then resumed proudly, 'I don't feel I can take anything more from you.'

'Can't or won't?' he asked.

She shrugged her shoulders. 'Does it make any difference?'

'No. I refuse to allow you to exist in near-poverty.'

Stung by his arrogant tone, she pointed out:

'I don't think it's anything to do with you any more. We've agreed to separate ...' She turned her head away, horrified to discover tears had risen to her eyes. He was just the same, magnetic, compelling, handsomer than she remembered him, and as unapproachable as during the last weeks of their association.

'Is there another man?' He shot the question at her so suddenly that she answered involuntarily:

'No, of course not.'

'Now that is surprising.' There was a sarcastic note in his voice. 'You've been gone about a year ... what have you been doing with yourself?'

'Oh, various things, but I feel it's time I took some regular employment, to give me an interest in life. It's not very satisfactory being just an idler.' She glanced at him uneasily. 'I don't know why you've come, Angelo. I understood you'd finished with me, and ... and ... it upsets me to re-open old wounds.'

She put her hand over her heart and looked at him reproachfully out of eyes like drowned violets.

'So that's how you feel about it? You want the past buried?'

'Don't you?'

He frowned, studying the point of his shoe.

'I happened to be in London, so I thought I would answer your letter orally. I wondered...' He broke off and gave her an oddly appealing look.

'You did at least read it,' she said bitingly.

Reminded of how he had treated her first epistle, he looked a little shamefaced.

'It was marked urgent and important,' he said defensively. 'Was it?'

'To me it was, but I hardly expected a personal call. How is Signora Verachi?'

She had hoped to disconcert him, but he merely shrugged his shoulders.

'The usual gossip has been at work, I see,' he observed. 'I paid her a little attention last winter. She is an amusing talker and we had a common interest in yachts, but if you think there was anything more——?' He looked at her accusingly.

'There probably was,' she returned flippantly. The Vera episode had caused her some pain.

His face froze. 'Believe what you please,' he said icily.

'But that's neither here nor there,' Francesca went on hastily, wishing she had not expressed her doubt. After all, she only had Maria's hints to go upon. 'We ... we've reached the point of no return, Angelo, you know that, and I want nothing more from you. I can manage very comfortably on my own earnings, and as far as I am concerned you are free as air.'

If only he would go before she broke down, crept on hands and knees to his feet, begging him to forgive her, to take her home again. The flat had never felt like home and England had become a land of exile. She yearned for blue sea and sky, the tall stems of the palms, the white villa above the coast, and this man whom she had learned to love too late.

She went on hardly: 'I thought Maria Donizetti was prepared to take my vacant place. You and she have so much in common, whereas you and I had nothing to say to each other.'

He sighed. 'Yes, I ought to have married her in the first place, instead of pursuing ... a dream.'

'Dreams are so unsatisfactory, aren't they?' she returned. 'One has to wake up.'

He looked at her searchingly, and she veiled her eyes with her lashes, fearing they might betray too much.

'You have not changed at all, have you, Francesca?' he told her a little bitterly. 'But I wish you to keep your allowance. After all, I owe you something for Bellavista. I believe it was to have been yours.'

She was silent, thinking it would be a comfort to have something behind her in case Angela or herself fell ill, and there would be her education later on. After all, he had a point about Bellavista, though the property would have been no use to her.

'Don't be too proud to accept it,' he said gently. 'Jobs can fall down and I could not bear to think of you in want.'

'Well, perhaps, for the time being,' she agreed, 'but won't two wives be somewhat expensive? I mean, if this dissolution goes through, you'll be marrying again.'

He stiffened, as if she had said something indiscreet.

'You view the prospect with equanimity?' he asked coldly.

Assuming with difficulty, because she was far from

doing so, an air of indifference, Francesca managed to shrug her shoulders and say carelessly:

'I understand it is inevitable, since you must have a son.'

He turned his eyes towards the window, his face inscrutable as he said: 'My father insists. On me lies the responsibility of carrying on our name.'

A reminder that Angela was useless for that purpose. A girl could not perpetuate the Vittorini family.

But he seemed reluctant, and Francesca surmised that he did not want to relinquish the bachelor life he found so alluring. Maria, she was sure, would put her foot down about that. But he did not look as if he had been enjoying himself. The gay exuberance that he had once possessed had vanished entirely.

He brought his gaze back from the window and on to her.

'Are you looking forward to your freedom, Francesca? There is some man after all?'

This time she was prepared. 'Perhaps,' she said archly.

His face darkened. 'I see, so maybe you will only need money ... for the time being. I hope you will not have to wait very long to be free, and I will keep you posted as to developments. So it is goodbye.' He hesitated, then added almost humbly: 'I am sorry I have messed up your life, Francesca.'

'So am I,' she concurred heartily. If she had never met him, never loved him, how different her life might have been; yet even while she formed the thought, she knew she was wrong. In spite of all she had suffered through him, she would never regret having known Angelo, and her love for him had widened and deepened her life.

He moved towards the door, and she watched him

with anguished eyes. This would be her last sight of him.

Angela woke and cried.

There is no mistaking the sound of a baby's wail, and Angela had good lungs. With his hand on the door knob, Angelo stood for an instant electrified. Then pushing Francesca aside, he strode into the bedroom to be greeted by Angela's roar.

Francesca followed, to find her daughter in her father's arms, and Angelo's eyes, furiously accusing, glaring at her over the downy black head.

Inadequately she said: 'You see, she was only a girl.'

'Only!' He looked down into the flower-like face, in which eyes, turning violet like her mother's, peered up at him vaguely. Angela liked the feel of her father's arms and having gained the attention that she desired, cooed.

Angelo sat down on the low chair beside the baby's cot, still holding the child.

'You dared to keep this from me,' he said to Francesca, in a low tense voice. 'All this while you have known, and never a hint, never a whisper! There, *poverina, amoretta, cuòre di mio cuòre*, I fear your mother is a very wicked woman.'

Francesca sat down upon her bed, feeling her legs would no longer support her. How could she have ever imagined Angelo would not want his daughter? A stab of fear went through her. Would he insist upon taking the child away from her?

'Is he so much to you, this other man?' Angelo asked. 'That you had to conceal this from me? Knowing that once I knew, I would never, never let you go?'

'There is no other man,' Francesca began, 'and...'
After all, she had tried to tell him and had her letter

returned.

He cut in before she could continue. 'Then *per Dio*, why, why? You are an enigma, Francesca. I doubt if you have any heart at all. First you try to run away from me on our wedding night and then you keep me from my child. *Dio*, how you must hate me!'

'I don't . . .' she began, but unheeding her, he went on. 'I tried so hard to win you, everything I had including my heart was yours. From the first moment I saw you, I wanted you, and you alone, but you were so cold, so aloof, and you believed everything bad you heard about me. All you ever desired was to get away from me.' His face hardened. 'But you have run your course. Even though you loathe me, you must come back now to raise your child. She is a Vittorini,' he glanced at the baby, 'no doubt of that, and she deserves something better than this . . . this hovel.' He looked at Francesca with infinite reproach. 'Did you forget that she is mine as well as yours?'

'No,' Francesca murmured, 'but it was all so difficult, and she wasn't the boy I knew you wanted.' Then at his puzzled frown, her conflicting emotions overcame her, and she flung herself down on the bed in a storm of tears.

Angelo laid the baby back in her cot, and turned to the weeping woman. He sat down beside her, but was careful not to touch her.

'Is the prospect of returning to Liguria so obnoxious to you?' he asked sadly. 'Even though I promise I will never lay a finger on you again?'

Francesca sat up, pushing back her tangled hair. 'Then . . . then we'll never have a son,' she said with a gulp, and threw herself into his arms.

It took Francesca some time to explain the complicity of emotions that had governed her conduct, and

186

she was hampered because she did not want to hurt Angelo by confessing how deeply she had misjudged him. Nor could he wholly understand her motives, and in retrospect, she was at a loss to understand them herself. How could she have believed Angelo was a reprobate, or doubted that he would want his daughter? Only two equally proud and sensitive natures could have contrived to misunderstand each other so lamentably.

'If I'd loved you less, I might have seen more clearly,' Francesca tried to explain, 'but if you'd told me that you loved me, which you never did, I wouldn't have been so stupid.'

'You didn't give me much opportunity,' he pointed out. 'At first I was afraid of scaring you, you were so withdrawn, and inclined to look upon me as a kind of monster. Oh, yes, you did,' as she tried to protest. 'If not the red devil, of close kin to him. At Cervo, I thought we were progressing, but Maria had to spoil it all. You thought I was a sort of Don Juan, didn't you? I pinned all my hopes upon our wedding night. I thought that at last I would be able to allay your fears. Well, you know what happened.' He smiled ruefully. 'Even a saint could be pardoned for being incensed when he caught his bride eloping. After that I feared I had antagonised you beyond forgiveness. The only hope left was that a child might draw us together.'

'But that letter,' she said. 'That cold, horrible letter.'

'I was very bitter when I wrote that,' he confessed. 'I felt I could never win your love, and since all you desired was to leave me the only thing I could do for you was to let you go, but I never dreamed you would deceive me about the child. You must have known by then.'

'Actually I didn't, not until I got to London, and

187

then when I thought how unsightly I would become, and all the things that might go wrong——' She buried her face in his shoulder.

'Idiot,' he said tenderly. 'Did you not know it was my privilege to sustain you at such a time? Francesca, *amore mia*, you have been very cruel to me.'

'I will do my best to make it up to you,' she whispered contritely.

With a touch of his old arrogance, he returned:

'I shall make sure you do.'

But Francesca, close in his arms, had no more misgivings, as she raised her face for his kiss.

Especially for you . . .

A Treasury of
HARLEQUIN ROMANCES

Golden
Harlequin Library

Many of the all time favorite Harlequin Romance Novels have not been available, until now, since the original printing. But now they are yours in an exquisitely bound, rich gold hardcover with royal blue imprint.

THREE COMPLETE UNABRIDGED NOVELS IN EACH VOLUME.

And the cost is so very low you'll be amazed!

Handsome, Hardcover Library Editions at Paperback Prices! ONLY $1.95 each volume

---

Start your collection now. See reverse of this page for brief story outlines.

To: HARLEQUIN READER SERVICE, Dept. G 412
      M.P.O. Box 707 Niagara Falls, N.Y. 14302
      Canadian address: Stratford, Ont., Canada

☐ Please send me complete listing of the 48 Golden Harlequin Library volumes.

☐ Please send me the Golden Harlequin Library editions I have checked.

I enclose $_____ (No C.O.D.'s) To help defray postage and handling costs, please add 50c.

NAME . . . .

ADDRESS . . . .

CITY/TOWN . . . .

STATE/PROV . . . . ZIP . . . .

Golden Harlequin $1.95 per vol.
Each Volume Contains 3 Complete Harlequin Romances

☐ Volume 13

DEAR SIR by Mary Burchell (No. 605)
Alexa found herself very attracted to Christopher, and she hoped with all her heart that he would never recall their first meeting. Then, quite suddenly he asked her "Were you ever in Paris?" . . . . so, he had remembered after all.

NURSE AT RYEMINSTER by Ivy Ferrari (No. 874)
Jenny Carr's complete concentration was devoted entirely to catching up with the full year's training which she had lost. When Dr. David Callender appeared on the scene, her attentions became — strangely diverted . . . .

THE BLUE CARIBBEAN by Celine Conway (No. 863)
When Ann Murray, with her brother and sister visited the exquisite Bahaman Island where her husband had left her an estate, the entire white population of Farando Kay was astonished at the three love stories which sprang up from the most unpromising of beginnings!

☐ Volume 18

MOUNTAIN CLINIC by Jean S. MacLeod (No. 638)
Elspeth's cousin Sybil found the peace of mind which she sought, in the lovely village of Grindelwald, in the Swiss Alps. When Elspeth's life touched that of a young Scots doctor, she too found serenity and contentment, the kind which only love brings . . . .

FORBIDDEN ISLAND by Sara Seale (No. 719)
Bewildered and angry, Lisa found herself virtually a prisoner of the dark, remote chieftain of a Highland clan. With each day that passed, on the little mist-encircled isle of Culoran, this gentle captivity became easier to bear.

DEAR FUGITIVE by Elizabeth Hoy (No. 573)
Susan had never considered the possibility that Iain might fall in love, not with her, but with her sister, Jan. In flower bedecked Edinburgh, at Festival time, a time of carefree delight, an "eternal triangle" is quickly taking shape . . . .

Golden Harlequin $1.95 per vol.

Each Volume Contains 3 Complete Harlequin Romances

☐ Volume 19

CHILD FRIDAY by Sara Seale (No. 896)
Friday's child is loving and giving, and this was Emily. But, was she loving enough to be of help to the blind embittered Dane Merritt, and giving enough to share herself with a child who had never known a warm-hearted affection?

HEART SPECIALIST by Susan Barrie (No. 587)
Dr. Daudet was reputed for his knowledge of the human heart. When, after long immunity his own heart was emotionally affected, by a shy young English girl, the famed Parisian specialist found himself learning all over again!

CHILDREN'S NURSE by Kathryn Blair (No. 633)
Linda's ideas on child care were quite different from the Marquez de Filano's, and this young English nurse's quiet obstinacy was a totally new experience for him. So, he began to study this girl — with an unexpected interest . . . .

☐ Volume 30

NURSE ON HOLIDAY by Rosalind Brett (No. 740)
Two gorgeous months of quiet, careless bliss, on the charming Mediterranean Island of Marganeta. Josie was going to enjoy this! Her troublesome brother and her stepmother were disturbing elements, but the real menace to her peace of mind was that dominating, dynamic character, Stuart Mendoza-Cortez Morland.

THE LAST OF THE LOGANS by Alex Stuart (No. 705)
Elizabeth Anson had once refused to marry him. His cousin Fiona bitterly resented his return. Nevertheless, Johnny was on his way from an Australian sheep station, to inherit the Highland home of his ancestors — and things were about to change!

COUNTRY OF THE HEART by Catherine Airlie (No. 789)
Jane had been ill. The post of nurse to a charming small boy on a cruise to the Canary Islands and North Africa was perfect. A series of adventures in the remote heart of Morocco, where east mingles with west ensues — was Jane quite fit to cope with all this excitement?

Golden Harlequin $1.95 per vol.
Each Volume Contains 3 Complete Harlequin Romances

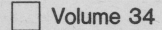 **Volume 34**

DEAR ADVERSARY by Kathryn Blair (No. 823)
Grant was an important man in the Copperbelt of Northern Rhodesia, he was used to managing people and things. When he tried to "manage" Morny Blake, she instinctively resisted him, for a woman will be mastered only — when she is loved.

CAMERON OF GARE by Jean S. MacLeod (No. 586)
Fiona Daviot and her father hated the Camerons. A relentless feud existed between the two families. Then, Fiona Daviot fell in love, with the last descendant of the hated race — Iain Cameron, but her father could not forgive!

DOCTOR MAX by Eleanor Farnes (No. 753)
Through Doctor Max Hartland's friendship and her work at the school for maladjusted children, Katrina's grief was subsiding. Then she discovered that Doctor Max Hartland was involved in the accident which killed her fiancee on the eve of their wedding!

Volume 35

NURSE AT CAP FLAMINGO by Violet Winspear (No. 884)
What was really a completely innocent situation, had looked rather compromising. So, to protect Fern's reputation, Ross had insisted on marrying her, but Fern was very much in love with him, and she wanted a better reason than that!

THE HOUSE OF ADRIANO by Nerina Hilliard (No. 840)
Duarte Adriano, Conde de Marindos was not only rich, but charming and handsome. Aileen found that he alternately attracted and annoyed her. The situation results in a colorful story, moving from Australia to Spain . . . .

THE DARK STRANGER by Sara Seale (No. 870)
A gypsy had predicted the coming of a dark stranger, and when Craig Pentreath entered Tina's life, she thought it might come true — but, the gypsy had not said that the coming of this stranger would bring Tina any happiness . . . .